All the dazzle and romance of courtly life are richly revealed in three sparkling tales from Camelot. They tell of spells and enchantments, wicked outlaws and hideous hags, maidens in distress and knights in shining armor. But most of all they tell of women and men in love, struggling to understand one another. King Arthur learns what women want more than anything else in the world. Geraint, the perfect knight, almost wrecks the perfect marriage. And the wizard Merlin meets his destiny and becomes a prisoner of love. With freshness and a sharp, contemporary wit, Winifred Rosen brings to life three timeless legends of Arthur and the Knights of the Round Table.

THREE
ROMANCES

Love Stories from Camelot Retold

BY WINIFRED ROSEN
Illustrated by Paul O. Zelinsky

ALFRED A. KNOPF, PUBLISHER

NEW YORK

For Rachel Sarah Garber

Library of Congress Cataloging in Publication Data

Rosen, Winifred, 1943–
  Three romances.

  Contents: The marriage of Sir Gawain and Dame
Ragnell—Enid and Geraint—Merlin and Niniane.
    1. Arthurian romances. [1. Arthur, King.
2. Knights and knighthood—Fiction. 3. Folklore—
England] 1. Zelinsky, Paul O. II. Title.
PZ8.1.R684Th 1981   823'.1'080351   81-5018
ISBN 0-394-84509-9   AACR2
ISBN 0-394-94509-3 (lib. bdg.)

THIS IS A BORZOI BOOK
PUBLISHED BY ALFRED A. KNOPF, INC.

CONTENTS

The

MARRIAGE

of

SIR GAWAIN

and

DAME

RAGNELL

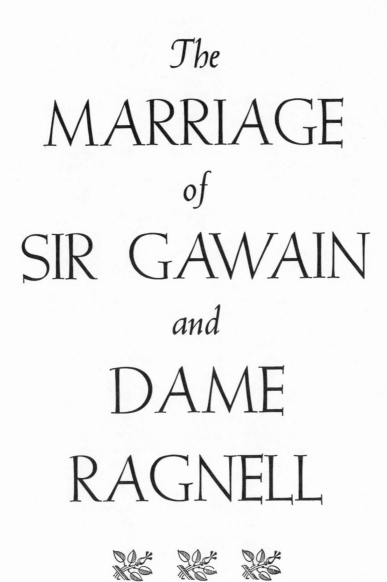

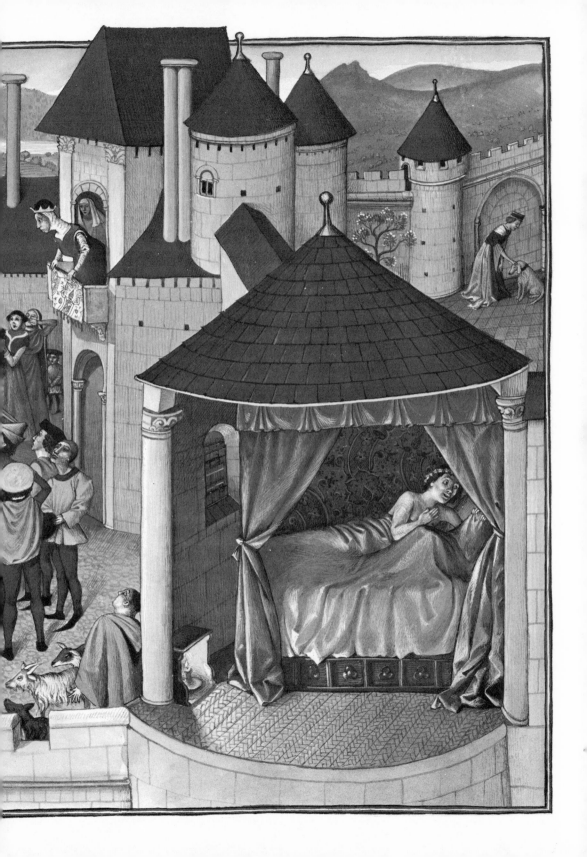

NE LOVELY SPRING DAY, KING ARTHUR WAS RIDING ahead of a small hunting party of knights when he came upon a deer. The animal fled and Arthur gave chase and finally killed it on the edge of a small clearing deep in the forest.

The King dismounted and flipped his reins over the bough of a tree. Then, drawing his hunting knife, he crouched among the ferns and proceeded to the dressing of the kill.

But suddenly a great shadow fell across the body of the beast lying before Arthur on the ground. The King turned to behold an armed and evil-looking knight, his sword drawn and ready to strike.

There was a moment of complete stillness. Arthur felt the blood freeze in his veins. Then the fierce knight spoke.

"Well, King Arthur," he said. "I am pleased to meet up with you at last. Many years ago, you did me a great wrong, and I have sworn that I would kill you if ever I got the chance."

Arthur stared up at the knight's grim, black-bearded face, but, try as he might, could not remember having seen the man before. That the stranger meant to murder him, however, he had no doubt. And so he did not hesitate to point out how dishonorable such a deed would be, and to assure the knight that it would ruin his reputation.

"Think about it," said the King. "You are in full armor with your weapon drawn, while I am defenseless and dressed only in my hunter's green."

Then he asked to know his would-be attacker's name.

"My name," said he, "is Sir Gromer Somer Joure."

This meant nothing to the King.

Evil though he was, Sir Gromer Somer Joure could not

deny that the King's point was well taken. And so, to preserve his knightly honor, he was forced to give in to some
degree. Still brandishing his sword, Sir Gromer Somer Joure
offered to spare the King's life temporarily, but only if Arthur
would agree to abide by certain conditions.

Arthur asked what these might be.

The knight replied that Arthur must solemnly swear to
return to the same spot one year from that day, alone and
unarmed, exactly as he was now, and to bring with him—in
exchange for his life—the correct answer to the following
riddle: *What do women want more than anything else in
the world?*

As a rule, Arthur was pretty good at riddles, but this one
stumped him. Indeed, it was the hardest riddle he had ever
heard, and it filled him with despair. But, knowing his life
would be worthless if he refused, Arthur agreed to the conditions.

Sir Gromer Somer Joure put away his sword. Then, after
reminding the King of his solemn pledge, he walked out of
the clearing and disappeared.

Arthur completed the dressing of the deer in a state of deep
distress.

Now, among the small company of knights who formed
the King's hunting party that day was Sir Gawain.

The King's nephew, Gawain was the brightest of the

bright-shining stars in Arthur's retinue; the finest, best-looking, most courageous and courteous knight in England.

When Arthur rejoined his knights, Gawain saw at once that the King was troubled. Drawing him aside, Gawain begged to know the reason for his dismay.

"I only hope that God will have mercy on me," Arthur sighed. "For I am afraid the days of my life are nearing an end." Then, swearing his nephew to secrecy, the King recounted all that had befallen him in the forest.

His nephew listened in grave silence until Arthur had finished. Then the two rode on some distance before Gawain spoke.

"It is certainly a most puzzling riddle," he admitted. "But you must not despair, Sire. I am sure we can find the answer in the course of a year."

Gawain pondered some more and then made the following suggestion: "Let each of us ride in different directions to distant lands, asking the question of everyone we meet. Then let us take all the answers and write them down in a great book that you can then present to Sir Gromer Somer Joure on the day of your appointment."

Arthur was deeply touched by Gawain's concern and by the love that had inspired so wise a plan. There was nothing, after all, in Arthur's contract with the wicked knight that prohibited him from bringing as many answers to the riddle as he chose, just as long as the correct answer was among them. And so, somewhat cheered, the King thanked Gawain from the bottom of his heart and agreed that they should do exactly as he had proposed.

❦

Unfortunately, many urgent problems, each demanding Arthur's personal attention, arose during the following months. For instance, a dragon appeared in the north, and although he was sure the ghastly stories about it were exaggerated, the King did not want people to panic, and so he undertook to slay the monster himself.

Then, too, the weather conspired against him. The early spring yielded to a killing frost that damaged many fruit trees and a large crop of spring wheat, which had just begun to sprout. Later, the hot winds of summer brought a parching drought. All over the kingdom streams and rivers dried up, pastures turned brown, and (most unfortunately!) the grapes withered on the vine.

Late in September, after a ruinous harvest, there was rain at last. But it brought little relief to Arthur's troubled realm, for no sooner had the heat wave passed than bands of outlaws began to roam the blighted countryside, plundering villages and holding up travelers on the highroad in broad daylight.

The King was very much occupied with affairs of state, and so the task of collecting answers to the riddle was left to his nephew, the loyal Sir Gawain.

Gawain spared no energy in the pursuit of his quest. Traveling tirelessly along highways and byways, through towns and villages, and into remote mountainous regions, he came upon many people. To each he asked his question: *What do women want more than anything else in the world?*

Everyone had an answer of one sort or another. Some said that women wanted good husbands; some declared they craved great wealth. Some thought women wanted fine clothing, but others were sure they cared only for respect. Gawain, who knew almost nothing about women, didn't think it was his place to judge the answers. And so, whether the replies seemed to him to be wise or foolish, he faithfully copied them all into the great, leather-bound book that he carried with him for this purpose.

✻

Finally, when only a month remained before the King's dreaded appointment with the terrible Sir Gromer Somer Joure, Gawain returned to court and presented Arthur with the book. "Sire," said Gawain, "this cannot fail to save your life."

A shaft of sunlight shining through a window high in the vaulted chamber lit up the knight's fair features and showed him to be aglow with strength and confidence. In truth, it was impossible for Gawain to imagine the King's death. He could more easily have imagined the sun falling out of the sky. And thus he had great faith.

But it was not so for the King.

The King had looked upon his death in the forest. He had seen its grim, black-bearded face. He had felt the blood freeze in his veins.

Since that moment, not a day had passed without Arthur's recalling every detail of the strange and terrible encounter. Nor had a night gone by without its being repeated in his dreams. And so, though he was deeply moved and even somewhat heartened by his nephew's confidence, the book did not put Arthur's mind entirely at ease. For he could not help wondering whether the correct answer really had been written there.

Nevertheless, he thanked Gawain with all his heart, saying, "If I had ten more lives to live, I could never find a more faithful friend than you have been."

Gawain replied, "Not so, Sire. For it is your goodness that inspires my devotion."

Rising, the King embraced his nephew, then asked his steward to serve Gawain food and drink and to see that all his needs and wishes were well attended to.

At dawn the next day, Arthur rode off alone, over hills and across meadows, until he came within sight of the forest. A carpet of lime-green grass and yellow daffodils covered the ground. In the trees buds were opening, birds singing. The dogwood was in bloom.

Never had the earth seemed more exquisite to the King than it did on that day. Except for a light veil of mist hugging the distant hilltops, the sky was bright blue, and warm winds blowing from the south carried the smells of flowers and the sea.

Arthur paused for a long time, seeing the beauty of the world as it can be seen only by someone who knows it soon may pass. The problems and cares that had so occupied his mind slowly vanished, like the morning mist from the hilltops. For a brief but precious moment, the King was aware only of the oneness and perfection of all things.

Then, suddenly, a cheerful tinkling of bells rang out from the direction of the forest. Arthur turned to see a mounted rider coming out of the trees.

At first glance, even from a distance, Arthur was surprised by the sight of the strange, stout figure coming toward him. But soon his surprise gave way to shock. Then horror. For, riding upon the back of a prancing, lily-white mare was the most hideous hag he had ever seen.

The hag's face was pocked and red; the end of her long, snotted snout hung over her lip, which was covered with bristling hairs. Two yellow tusks—one curling up, the other down—grew out of the corners of her gaping mouth, and great rolls of wrinkled fat hung down from her grizzled chin. Ugly cannot begin to describe her; she was loathsome, foul. And, of course, she was far from clean.

Now Arthur had seen many terrible things in his day (a huge serpent, for example, with black venomous fangs the length of a man's hand), but he had never seen anything as grotesque as the hideous creature who now stopped by his side and addressed him directly.

"Greetings, King Arthur. It is well we've met!"

This was hardly a sentiment shared by the King. In fact, he had a tremendous urge to gallop away as fast as he could. But he resisted it and returned the old hag's greeting with due courtesy.

"Do not doubt your good fortune," she told him cheerfully. "For without my help you are a dead man."

Amazed, the King stared at her.

"You see," she said with a wink, "I know all about the riddle. I also know that none of the answers you have found will save your life. Luckily, I can help you. But first you must promise me one thing."

"Anything!" exclaimed the King. "Just tell me who you are, and—if my life is really in your hands—you can have whatever you want, I swear."

"My name," she told him, "is Dame Ragnell. And I will make a fair bargain with you. If your life is not saved by my answer, you shall be released from your promise. But if my answer serves and your head is not lost, you must honor your pledge."

The King told her to name her desire.

And she did. "I want the finest knight in the kingdom for my husband. I would wed your nephew, the noble Sir Gawain."

"God's mercy upon me!" cried the King, horrified by her suggestion. And he hastened to inform her that even if he wanted to, it would be beyond his power to make such a pledge. "It is Gawain's right to decide for himself whom he will marry," the King explained.

Whereupon the hag advised Arthur to hurry home and put her proposal before Gawain himself. "And do try to be convincing," she advised. "For though I may be horrible to look at, I am very gay at heart!"

Then she turned the mare's head and trotted off, the bells on her harness tinkling merrily.

⚜

Although the sun was now high in the sky, the King rode home in profound darkness. Only when he heard the clattering of his horse's hooves on the wooden drawbridge crossing the moat did he begin to be aware of the world of shapes and colors, the faces of the guards on duty at the gatehouse, the alley—momentarily blocked by a herd of goats—leading through an archway into the castle keep.

Passing through the archway, the King glanced up automatically to where the lookouts were posted high on the castle's towers. All was in order. He rode slowly through the outer courtyard, around the mews, and past the kennels. With ever-increasing anguish in his heart, he approached the stables.

Gawain was waiting for him there, his hair as gold as a field of wheat in the sunlight. Before the King had even dismounted, the youth was again begging to know the reason for his ill-concealed distress.

Arthur described his meeting with Dame Ragnell and told Gawain of her proposal.

Gawain replied without a second's delay. "Sire, I beg you to return at once and bring her my most solemn pledge of marriage!"

But Arthur would not hear of it. "The extent of her ugliness is indescribable," he told his nephew. "She is foul beyond words, beyond thoughts!"

"But, Sire, I would gladly give my *life* for you," Gawain declared.

They were silent for a moment. Then Arthur asked, "Do you remember that warty old crone we once met—the one who dwelled in the bat cave high in the hills?"

Gawain remembered her.

"Well, she was a *prize* compared with the creature I am telling you about."

But this made no difference to Gawain, who insisted he would marry the hag happily, were she a fiend from hell itself.

Though passionate, the King's arguments were all in vain. Finally he gave in, saying: "Of all my knights, Gawain, you are the flower!" Then he turned his horse and wearily rode back to the forest.

※

Arthur met again with Dame Ragnell in the same spot as before, and when he gave her not only his own pledge but also Gawain's, her delight was disgusting to behold. Her drooling grin and the excited trembling of her flesh were so repulsive that, even though he had seen many terrible things in his day, Arthur felt a little faint.

Then the hag said, "Now, King Arthur, you shall hear what you need to know. And, though it may astonish you, my answer will not fail to save your life, for it is the truth. The one thing women want more than they want anything else in the world is to be given *sovereignty*. That is their dream, their desire, and their fantasy."

"Sovereignty?" whispered the astonished King.

She nodded.

"It cannot be!" exclaimed Arthur, for the idea was contrary to all his beliefs and therefore disturbed him greatly.

Like most men, Arthur believed that women wanted to be ruled by men, to be subject to their laws and protection—just as men wanted to be ruled and protected by their government, to be subject to the will of their King, their sovereign.

Arthur believed that women were prizes to be won, precious objects to be seized, guarded, used, admired. Not only that, he believed that women thought of themselves the same way

—as subject beings whose purpose in life was to give men pleasure. In the King's mind, this was the natural order of things, and try as he might, he could not imagine them otherwise.

The hag replied as if she had been reading his thoughts. "Things are not always what they pretend to be, King Arthur. But, whether or not you believe it, your life will be saved by my answer—which, by the way, I have risked much to tell you. For the cruel knight will be enraged when you say it, and he will curse me knowing that I am the only one who could have told it to you."

Having obtained the hag's answer at such a terrible price, the King was hard-pressed to feel any gratitude toward her. Nevertheless, he thanked her as courteously as he could before spurring his horse in the direction of his castle.

"God be with you, King Arthur," called the hag as he rode away. "And remember: I'll be waiting right here on the day of your appointment!"

"It's impossible! How can women want *us* to give *them* sovereignty! The idea is ridiculous!" Arthur paced up and down the length of the stable muttering to himself.

Gawain looked on compassionately. He knew that too much depended on the hag's answer for the King to judge it fairly. Not only was it contrary to all Arthur's beliefs and upsetting to his notion of the natural order of things, but the answer, if correct, threatened his favorite knight with a terrible fate. So Gawain was not surprised to hear that Arthur refused to believe it.

As for Gawain, he had one desire and one desire only: to save the King's life. He did not care how this was accomplished or how great a sacrifice he would have to make. And since he knew next to nothing about women himself, he wisely reserved judgment on the answer.

The King's agitation was upsetting the horses; they snorted and stamped their feet as he passed their stalls. But Arthur seemed not to notice. He was in a terrible state, torn between conflicting emotions, his mind caught like a beast in a trap: the more he struggled, the more suffering it caused him.

Gawain tried to calm him saying, "Do not despair, Sire. After all, a whole month remains before your appointment."

Imagining a month of tortured days and sleepless nights, the King was not cheered by this observation.

Then Gawain said, "So far, in the interests of security, we have refrained from putting the riddle to anyone at court. Let us refrain no longer. Truly, there is no wiser or more worldly group of men than the knights of King Arthur's Round Table. Surely one of them is bound to come up with a better answer than any we have yet been given."

The King felt a sudden glimmering of hope. He stopped pacing, looked up, and said, "Of course. Maybe Tristram would know—he has certainly been around—or else Lancelot.

Percival, of course, has never looked at a woman in his life, so he's not likely to be much help, but Mordred has had more than enough experience for two. Yes, it is a good plan, Gawain. We will do as you say."

❀

During the weeks that followed, Gawain and the King approached the other knights of the Round Table, and being careful not to arouse their suspicions, asked each one of them, *What do women want more than anything else in the world?*

First they asked Tristram, who said, "What women want most is to be softly caressed."

Lancelot thought they preferred to be gorgeously dressed.

"To be warm and well fed," said another.

"To be always in bed," winked his brother.

Every knight had a ready answer. Unfortunately, they were not very different from the answers Gawain and Arthur had heard before. Nevertheless, Gawain carefully wrote each one down in the great, leather-bound book. And, though the King grew more anxious than ever, Gawain still felt sure that things would turn out well in the end.

❀

On the day of his appointment with Sir Gromer Somer Joure, the King rode out alone from his castle, wearing his tunic and breeches of hunter's green.

The splendid spring had reached its peak. Sunlight lay like

liquid gold upon the gently curving stems of feathered grass in the flower-sprinkled meadows, and the hills were purple with heather. Although the sun had warmed the early morning air, a film of dewdrops still clung to the surfaces of things, making the earth look as if it had been created only a moment or two before.

However, hurrying his horse in the direction of the forest, the King saw everything as though at a great distance, as in a dream. Nothing seemed real enough to touch him, not even the sun. He was icy cold.

He galloped onward. Startled birds flew into the air; rabbits dashed across the fields in zigzag patterns, madly fleeing his approach.

Entering the forest, the King again started a deer. But this time he did not chase it.

His enemy was waiting.

"Welcome, King Arthur," said the evil-looking knight, drawing his sword as Arthur rode up.

The King nodded and returned a formal greeting. Then he dismounted, hitched his horse to a tree, and, armed only with his leather-bound book, strode into the middle of the clearing.

When the two were face to face, the knight asked Arthur for his answer to the riddle. And the King, being unwilling to give the answer he had gotten from the hag at so terrible a price (an answer that in any case could not possibly be right), presented him with the book.

As Sir Gromer opened the volume and read down the first page of answers, a cruel, self-satisfied smile twisted his bloodless lips. He said, "If this is as good as you've got, you're no better than dead."

He laughed then, a sharp, cold laugh that cut right through the King's flesh, stopping his heart and chilling him to the bone. Nevertheless, Arthur invited Sir Gromer to read on.

The knight did so. But the cruel smile never left his lips, and he looked up every now and then to laugh out loud.

Several hours passed. By the time the knight had finished reading, it was nearly noon.

Shutting the book, he said, "You must have gone to a great deal of trouble to get all these answers. Too bad none of them is right."

"Are you sure?" asked Arthur.

"None of them even comes *close*," Sir Gromer assured him.

"I was afraid of that," sighed the King.

Then the knight raised his sword, saying, "I only hope you're not afraid to die, King Arthur, for you are about to."

"Wait!" cried the King.

"For what?"

"I still have one more answer."

"You try my patience!" complained Sir Gromer, reluctantly lowering his sword. "But, as it is no doubt as wrong as the others I read, go on, say it . . . then I'll cut off your head!" And he laughed his heartless laugh.

Arthur, looking very pale, hesitated. He had to speak, of

course, for a King's first duty was to save his life by any means. Still, if the answer turned out to be true, Gawain's fate would be too miserable to contemplate. Nevertheless, Arthur took a deep breath, drew himself up very straight, and repeated the answer he had heard from the hag: "There is one thing above all others that women want. It is their dream, their desire, and their fantasy to have *sovereignty* over men."

He paused again, then added, a little apologetically: "Naturally, I find the idea hard to take seriously, but the person I heard it from swore it would save me."

Whereupon, a look of violent rage swept over the evil knight's grim features, and he cursed the name of Dame Ragnell again and again. He also uttered many terrible profanities such as would be unseemly to repeat as they were all in extremely bad taste.

The King, of course, was greatly relieved. But before he could say anything, his enemy—the very wicked and now equally disappointed Sir Gromer Somer Joure—turned on his heel, marched out of the clearing, and disappeared.

Arthur's happiness was short-lived. The hag was waiting for him at the edge of the forest.

Smiling grotesquely, she expressed great joy to see him alive and well, and though Arthur couldn't honestly return the compliment, he managed to acknowledge her with civility. Together they rode back to the castle where he knew Gawain would be anxiously awaiting him.

Their arrival caused quite a stir, for of course it shocked everyone to see such a hideous creature riding so gaily into the castle right behind the King. No one had ever seen—or even imagined—anyone as ugly as Dame Ragnell before, and naturally they all wanted to get a closer look. And so a large crowd gathered and followed them into the courtyard.

This made Arthur deeply ashamed, for he did not like to be seen in public with such a hideous companion. And who can blame him?

As for Gawain, he was so overjoyed to see his uncle alive that at first he was not even aware of the other's presence. But as the crowd grew larger and the hubbub in the courtyard increased, Gawain's attention was inevitably drawn to the object of so much excitement and curiosity.

Fortunately, the hag was partly hidden and a fair distance away. Even so, Gawain felt a little faint. But because he knew her to be the instrument of his uncle's salvation, he got a grip upon himself. Taking deep breaths, he threaded his way through the crowd to the empty space in the center of the courtyard and gallantly knelt before her on the ground. Then, addressing the hag as his wife-to-be, he welcomed her to Camelot in the most gracious and courteous terms, loud enough for everyone to hear.

A moment of strained and unnatural silence followed Gawain's speech. Then he stood up and as he moved forward to help the hag down from her horse, a loud groan of horror and dismay rose from the assembly.

Now, being the bravest, best-looking, and most courteous knight in all England, Gawain was naturally a great favorite at court, especially with the ladies, all of whom adored him passionately and would have married him in a moment. Hearing him pledge his troth to the hideous hag was more than they could bear. A number of women who had been standing nearby actually passed out cold; others gasped and fell to their knees, sobbing hysterically.

Luckily, none of this bothered Dame Ragnell a bit so pleased was she with the courteous way Gawain had received her.

Hopping down from her white palfrey—she was surprisingly light on her feet—she curtsied merrily and said, "Heavens, Gawain! I wish for your sake I were a beautiful woman, for you are a true Man among Men."

Gawain knew she meant well, but her wish was so tragically far from the repulsive truth that he couldn't help feeling depressed. Everything about her was loathsome: her filthy hair matted into rats' nests; the boar's tusks protruding from her hairy mouth; her thick neck; and her heavy, drooping breasts. She was, he thought, as far from beautiful as it is possible to get.

Nevertheless, not for a moment did he let the hag's grotesqueness prevent him from being absolutely courteous and correct.

As he escorted her toward the castle, a loud wailing went up from the women, and quite a few men broke down and openly wept.

※

King Arthur hoped to postpone the wedding for a while, but Dame Ragnell would not hear of it. She wanted to be married at once. Nor would she be put off with a quiet wedding but insisted on an elaborate ceremony, to be followed by a feast in the main hall.

At the feast, she ate well. She ate, in fact, everything in sight, including several chickens, a whole rack of lamb, and two suckling pigs—tearing at the food with her tusks and fingernails, devouring every last shred of flesh until only a heap of bones remained.

Needless to say, everyone's appetite was ruined.

The King drank heavily.

It was a dismal affair.

When the feast ended, it was Gawain's duty to take his bride off to bed.

Sick and in a kind of daze, Gawain led the way down several corridors and up a stone staircase to the wing of the castle where the bridal chamber was kept. The journey seemed to take forever, for the hag was staggering under the weight of her recent meal, and Gawain's heart was so heavy with dread that merely to put one foot in front of the other took every ounce of strength he had.

The bridal chamber was furnished with a big bed and very

little else. The bed was hidden behind thick draperies, but Gawain knew that it was there, and this fact made him more miserable than he'd ever been in his life.

As he undressed in the dark, the knight could not help wishing that he were anywhere but where he was, with any other duty—no matter how dangerous—to perform.

Trembling violently, he knelt down and said his prayers. Then he rose, quietly parted the curtains, and slipped into bed, wishing he'd never even been born.

Inside the curtained bridal bed, it was dark and as silent as a tomb. It was a very big bed, but Gawain lay stretched out straight as a jousting lance along the very edge, facing the curtains, hardly daring to breathe. He desperately hoped, of course, that the hag, having feasted so extravagantly, was already falling asleep. For Gawain was never without hope. Another hope he had was that if he could just get through this one, terrible night, things would be better in the morning.

So deep was the silence that Gawain could hear the quick, rhythmic beating of his heart. Time passed slowly—but pass it did, and, little by little, Gawain's hope grew.

Then, all of a sudden, he was startled by a rustling noise— the sound of a curtain parting behind him. His heart sank like a stone. For he realized that his hope had been a dream: the hag was not asleep at all! In fact, she was just now getting into bed.

Gawain felt himself plunging from the height of his foolish

fancy into the depths of despair. Then, as the hag heaved her great weight onto the bed, another hope—like a friendly hand —reached out to save him. Maybe if he stayed perfectly still, she'd think *he'd* fallen asleep. Surely it was worth a try. . . .

For a long while he didn't move, didn't breathe, didn't even think.

Just as it seemed his plan had succeeded, the hag tapped him on the shoulder and said, "Who do you think you are fooling, Gawain? I know you're not asleep."

And the youth started up so violently he nearly fell out of bed.

She said, "You see? I knew you wouldn't behave so discourteously to me. After all, I am your wife. And you know what *that* means."

Gawain stammered out a weak denial, but the hag would have none of it.

"Come, Gawain. We all know how pure you are in heart and deed, but a knight your age cannot be totally ignorant. By now you must have an *idea,* a general-if-foggy impression of what your duty is to me."

Gawain had never lied to anyone in his life, and he didn't want to start now—even if it would do any good, which he doubted. In truth, he did have a sort of general idea, a foggy kind of impression concerning the nature of the duty she had just mentioned. And it filled him with unspeakable dread.

He lay there neither speaking nor moving. In the first

place, he couldn't, for the life of him, think of anything to say. And, although he wished he could move—turn over on his back at least, for he knew he was being very rude—the thought of the hag's repulsive snout, bristling hairs, and dangerous tusks made him want to leap out of the bed so badly that it was all he could do to stay right where he was.

"Sir Gawain, I am offended by your coldness," complained the hag.

This distressed the knight exceedingly, for it was a strict point of honor with him never to offend anyone, least of all a lady, though he had some doubt as to whether Dame Ragnell qualified as that. But it didn't matter what you called her, he thought. She had saved his Uncle Arthur's life! The knight was stung by remorse.

"The reason for your coldness is obvious," said the hag sadly. "You are put off by my ugliness."

He couldn't deny it.

"You would not act this way if I were beautiful," she sighed.

Gawain thought, "If she were plain—*unattractive,* even. But, God have mercy! She is so unthinkably foul! Uncle Arthur was right, she makes the bat-cave lady look like a prize."

"The problem," Dame Ragnell was saying, "is that I am not really your wife until you love me the way you agreed to —*vowed* to, in fact, before God and everybody. It's true I am a hideous old hag, but I did save the King's life, remember. So, for Arthur's sake, you might kiss me at least. One kiss, Gawain—is that too much to ask?"

The mention of his Uncle Arthur did it. "No!" cried the knight, suddenly beside himself with guilt. "It is *not* too much to ask."

"Then you will do it?"

"No! I mean, *yes*—I shall do more! By heaven, I swear it. I shall act according to my vow—" So saying, he turned, intending to take the hideous hag in his arms. But, facing her, he beheld instead: *the most beautiful woman he had ever seen!*

Truthfully, beautiful cannot begin to describe her. She was exquisite beyond belief, a vision in a dream: flesh smooth as the petals of a rose, hair swirling like river water all about her.

Gawain was struck as though by a blow from a sword. Piercing his body, she entered his soul. He seemed to die and —in the same instant—to be reborn.

Many moments passed, but the youth remained motionless, staring at the enchanted form before him, unable to believe his eyes. Finally, in a voice so low that it sounded like the wind in the trees, the lady asked Gawain what he was waiting for.

He took a deep breath, and the sweet smell of jasmine in the air made him suddenly lightheaded. "Who *are* you?" he asked.

"Why," she said with a smile, "what a strange question! I am your wife, of course, just as I was before."

"Oh. I didn't recognize you," said Gawain, who still was not quite master of his wits.

Her laughter fell like spring rain, gently and refreshingly sweet. "Sir knight, you are unkind," she murmured.

Gawain begged the lady to forgive him. "But it's all so terribly confusing," he explained. "For now you are beautiful beyond measure, whereas before you appeared hideous in my sight. However, nevermind. To have you as you are now gives me indescribable delight!"

And with these words, he took her in his arms, and together they made great joy.

But, when the night had nearly passed and darkness was giving way to dawn, the lady spoke again. "Sir knight, it grieves me to have to tell you this, but my beauty is only temporary; it will not hold for more than half the day. The other half, I'm afraid, I will be as I was before. Now, you must choose how you would have me: beautiful by day before all men's eyes and hideous at night; or hideous by day and beautiful only in your sight."

Needless to say, this news distressed Gawain deeply. He wondered if it would have been better not to have been born at all rather than face such a terrible choice.

Neither alternative appealed to him, to say the least. For while he rejoiced at the idea of seeing his lady in the daylight, the thought of having to share his bed with the scabrous old hag made him wretched. On the other hand, if his wife were beautiful at night, his days would be a nightmare.

He pondered at length, trying to see the problem from every point of view. But, no matter how much he thought about it, he could not decide which possibility was the better, or at least the less lamentable, of the two.

And so he said, "Truly, I cannot tell whether it would be best to have you beautiful at night and foul during the day, or foul by day and beautiful at night. And so, dear lady, let it be as you would wish. I leave the choice in your hands. For my heart, my body, and everything I have belongs to you."

Whereupon she cried out: "May God bless you, most noble and courteous knight! For your answer has released me from an evil spell. *Henceforth I will be beautiful all the time!*"

And then she recounted how, long ago, she had spurned the advances of the evil Sir Gromer Somer Joure, who then enchanted her. "He condemned me to remain in my loathsome shape until such time as the finest knight in the kingdom would marry me and yield to me sovereignty over himself and all that he possessed. And you have just done so, thank God!"

Hearing this, Gawain was in ecstasy. Once again, words failed him.

But his lady did not mind a bit. Holding out her arms, she cried, "Kiss me, Sir Gawain! And together let us make joy."

This time, the knight needed no convincing. He kissed her.

And together they made joy out of mind.

ENID

and

GERAINT

I.

THE KNIGHTS WHO JOINED TOGETHER UNDER KING Arthur's rule to form the fellowship of the Round Table were all marvelous men. Each and every knight was marvelous in his own right, independently of the others. But when the knights formed their alliance, their powers increased immensely, and they came to seem almost like gods.

Geraint, Prince of Devon, was one of Arthur's most splendid knights; a star in the constellation of the fellowship who shone with special brilliance, even among the dazzling lights of his companions. For, though there were a few men whose daring exploits brought them more renown, no one was more constant, more unwavering in his devotion to the King's cause than Sir Geraint, the Lord of Devon.

Geraint was married to Enid, the only daughter of Duke Ynoil, and Geraint's love for her was beyond the power of words to measure. As a field in springtime loves the light on which its life depends, so did Devon's Lord adore his lady. Nor did his passion alter with the changing seasons; even after they had been married for a full year, Geraint awoke every day at dawn and, seeing Enid's face, diamondlike against her coal-black curls, he felt the same startled wonder as when her beauty first broke upon him. He would gaze at Enid as she slept, drinking in the sight of her the way a thirsty man drinks water from a pool.

Enid gave her husband just as freely of her love, and however much she gave him, her heart was always full, its source constantly replenished. Therefore was their happiness complete, and for a whole year they made great joy at all times.

※

But on the eve of the Great Fall Tournament, Geraint overheard a remark that changed his life completely.

His groom having been undone by the festivities of the

night before, Geraint, full of sympathy for the lad, was seeing to his horse himself when he heard a group of young,
unmarried knights conversing upon the subject most favored
by their kind, namely, the conquest of ladies.

The sons of wealthy lords, the visiting youths were extremely well endowed; they were rich, good-looking, and
quick-witted. All they lacked, unfortunately, was humility,
and as for discretion, they did not know the meaning of the
word, especially when it came to the subject they were
presently discussing.

As he listened to their talk, Geraint recalled how arrogant
he himself had been at their age, and was amazed to realize
how much his attitude had changed. These days, he neither
looked at nor thought about ladies at all. Except for Enid, of
course, whom he regarded with awe and thought about with
the utmost reverence.

It amused him, therefore, to listen to these callow youths
talk as if they knew it all. To hear them speak, you would
think no lady was safe from their charms; all they had to do
was whisper a few flatteries, give her a trinket or two, and—
Presto!—the wench was in their power. Any fool could do it.
Why if anything, it was too easy. For the fun was in the
conquest; as soon as a damsel's heart was won, she ceased to
be of interest to them. Unless, of course, she lived in some
very remote place or, better yet, was married.

Though all ladies were fair game, married ladies were by

far the fairest in the young men's estimation. Illicit affairs were the most intriguing, and with married ladies there was less danger of anything untoward happening. Whereas if a maiden were to be dishonored, certain pressures would be brought to bear, and none of the young men could see any advantage in they themselves getting married just then.

Little heeding the Prince, who seemed preoccupied with his charger, the youths went on talking for some time. And the longer they did so, the more spirited their discussion became, until they went so far as to begin listing the names of the damsels whose hearts they claimed to have conquered. As this was most unchivalrous to the Prince's way of thinking, he decided to reprimand them. But, just then, one of the youths said something so scandalous that it took his breath away. For the remark concerned no less a lady than Guenevere, the Queen!

Now slanderous gossip was hardly unheard of at Camelot. Indeed, scandal was always in the air—like the smell of honeysuckle in spring—and thus no one took it too seriously. But this was slander of an altogether different variety. The Queen had been charged with infidelity! Supposedly she lusted after King Arthur's foremost knight and dearest friend, the great Sir Lancelot—and Lancelot, it seems, was equally enamoured of the Queen.

Geraint, enraged by the accusation, lunged for the throat of the youth who had spoken, thus startling his stallion and creating no end of panic, noise, and confusion. Fortunately, the other knights prevented the Prince from strangling their companion. Geraint was finally prevailed upon to accept the young man's apology, provided that he and his friends would swear, on pain of death, never to refer to the evil rumor, even to one another. Fearing the Prince's vengeance, the young men swore never to mention the incident again.

But the sad affair did not end there. Geraint was too deeply distressed by the idea of the Queen's faithlessness. He found it disgraceful, unspeakable, *unthinkable!* But not, alas, impossible.

※

That the Queen and Lancelot were indeed madly in love is a tragedy no one can deny, for it became common knowledge in time. But since there was as yet no evidence to support it, the idea was really far-fetched and might easily have been dismissed by Geraint as nonsense. Nevertheless, for some reason he did not understand himself, the Prince believed it immediately. And it caused him much pain and suffering.

The Queen's lust for Lancelot would, in itself, have grieved the Prince. But the thought that Enid—his own wife—was the Queen's closest friend and most trusted confidante added considerably to his misery.

The two ladies had liked each other from the moment they met, and had indeed become quite intimate. Although Enid's official position was that of lady-in-waiting to the Queen, Guenevere treated her more like a sister. And Geraint had found this very gratifying; in fact, he had taken pains to encourage the friendship right from the start. However, the more he thought about that now, the sicker he felt at heart.

Let no one suppose that Enid was in any way at fault for the awful ordeal that was to follow. Nothing she had ever said or done was the least bit deserving of reproach. She was purer even than the driven snow. Truly, everyone thought so.

But Geraint was not heartened by the thought of Enid's purity. Indeed, her virtue was a disadvantage, he decided, as he left the stables and threaded his way in a daze across the busy courtyard. In faith, she believed everyone was as virtuous and high-minded as she. Geraint had considered this one of her finest qualities before, but suddenly, he wasn't so sure. Now it occurred to him that she was defenseless against evil and might be tainted merely by association with the Queen.

"Why, she worships the very ground beneath Guenevere's feet!" he told himself.

Because he was upset, Geraint was exaggerating things— imagining Enid to be even better than she was, while making the Queen out to be some sort of fiend. In the state he was in, it seemed to him that everything must be either one way or the other—right or wrong, good or evil—which proves how distressed he was, for, as he knew very well, things are rarely that simple.

But the idea of the Queen's infidelity troubled him deeply. Then, too, his mind was uneasy about the coming tournament. Geraint had an illustrious reputation to maintain, and he was sure to be challenged by every up-and-coming young knight eager to win instant renown by vanquishing the Prince of Devon before so large and distinguished a crowd.

And so Geraint's thoughts became increasingly confused. By turns, he grew suspicious and afraid. And by the time he crossed the courtyard and entered the washhouse, he had decided that Enid's trusting nature had placed her in grave danger and that he alone could save her.

Meanwhile, Enid was thoroughly enjoying herself at a reception being held in the Queen's chambers.

As you would expect on the eve of such a great event, Guenevere was entertaining a number of important guests— and entertaining them royally, for she had a flair for that sort of thing. Her elegant apartments were festooned with flowers and furnished with precious ornaments and splendid tapestries all intricately intertwined with fantastical birds and beasts. Laughter and the music of lutes filled the air; a troupe of acrobats delighted the assembly with feats of amazing agility. Though the sun had just begun to set, Guenevere had ordered all the torches lit, and the scene, drenched in shimmering golden light, was almost unreal, as if Merlin had magically created it.

Geraint, now washed and dressed, made his way through the maze of crowded corridors to the Queen's apartments. By this time he had worked himself into a dreadful state. He was obsessed by the awful thought: the Queen and Lancelot! Lancelot and the Queen! Like bells, the words tolled incessantly in his brain.

The Queen and Lancelot! He should have suspected it. Now that he did, it seemed so obvious. Guenevere had always favored Lancelot. Indeed, she treated him with more than courtesy. In fact, it would not be unfair to say that she treated him affectionately, more affectionately, come to think of it, than she had been treating her husband of late.

O that the noble Arthur should be so betrayed!

It was too much for Geraint. Momentarily overcome, he paused in the empty corridor and prayed to God, begging His mercy on the King. Then he parted the heavy draperies and entered the reception room.

Enid was speaking gaily to Guenevere and Lancelot—she'd never been to a Fall Tournament and could hardly contain her excitement. Geraint's appearance, like a gust of wind foretelling bad weather, startled her. She stopped talking at once, seized by the impulse to leap up and rush to her husband's side. She halfway rose, but—checked by his strange, almost menacing look—sank back again, confused.

Observing her, the Prince instantly suspected the worst: Enid was already aware of the conspiracy between Guenevere and Lancelot.

Geraint rode badly in the tournament—indeed, he came perilously close to disgracing himself during the course of the day. Twice he was nearly unhorsed by adversaries of inferior rank and ability; and once he actually dropped his lance while turning about, which meant he had to forfeit the rest of the joust. Though his body was sorely abused, that was nothing compared with the damage to his dignity. He was mortified by his performance, as he had every right to be.

Geraint was not one of those knights who delights in combat for its own sake, seizing the slightest grievance as an excuse to fight to the death. No, that was not, and never had been, Geraint's way. As a Prince, he preferred whenever possible to settle disputes by peaceful means; he was famous for his even temper, sound judgment, and diplomacy. Still, his bravery and strength were legendary. He would not have hesitated to defend with his life any just cause, nor to inflict serious harm or even death on anyone he knew to be his enemy.

The Prince was a fine horseman and a master of weaponry. Besides being wonderful to look upon, he was intelligent, sober, and considerate. The King, moreover, placed great value on his services, for he knew him to be devoted to the sacred cause of Chivalry, whose high ideals the Knights of the Round Table were sworn to defend.

And so, it is no wonder that Geraint was mortified by his poor performance that day. Though the tilts and jousts were

fought with blunted weapons, according to the rules of sports-
manship, the knights did not consider them games. They did
not fight for the fun of it, in other words, but to prove their
True Worth as Men. What is more, the Knights of the Fellowship competed fiercely among themselves, for each was
eager to prove himself superior to his comrades.

This was hardly in keeping with the spirit of the Round
Table, which had been created by Arthur (at Merlin's suggestion) to eliminate differences in rank and discourage the
knights from fighting among themselves. The members of
Arthur's fellowship were acknowledged to be the finest
knights in England, and they were all, supposedly, equal in
power and prestige. But in reality, it was a different story.
Arthur's knights had always been competitive, and now that
the Kingdom was well established and there were no major
wars to engage them, their rivalry was intense.

Despite Geraint's defeat, the tournament was a great suc-
cess. The weather was glorious: sunny and clear with just
enough of a breeze to keep the horses happy and the pennants flying. Arthur's knights rode with great distinction,
easily defeating every challenger. Lancelot rode with far more
distinction than anyone, for Lancelot, of course, had the
strength of ten.

Geraint, though mortified by his performance, said nothing to anyone about what was bothering him. Truly, the possibility of confiding in someone never even occurred to him,

and he would have rejected it as unmanly if it had. So no one, not even his closest comrades, knew what to make of his disgraceful performance in the games that day. Nor could he be prevailed upon to enlighten them in any way.

As for Enid, she could only thank God when the tournament ended that Geraint had not come to serious harm.

As the days passed, however, she grew more and more alarmed. For, instead of improving, the Prince's spirits steadily declined. The signs of his distress were every day more obvious. He was listless and rarely spoke; he ate but little, and as he could not seem to fall asleep, took to drinking more than was his custom. And so, because Enid loved Geraint better than life itself, she grew more distressed with every passing day.

※

Enid was every bit as beautiful as she was good. Her face, though thin and somewhat angular, was soft, the skin as lustrous as the inside of a seashell. Despite the delicacy of her features, her lips were sufficiently full to warrant being called sensual, while her blue-grey eyes could fairly be likened to two birds flying off into space. What is more, she had masses of coal-black curls such as no lady could fail to envy, nor any lord ignore.

For all her endowments, however, Enid was not vain. On the contrary, she was an excellent person—a woman who possessed virtue, beauty, and intelligence to such an extent that she was regarded by many at court as a perfect example of what a woman ought to be, as defined by the high ideals of Chivalry.

Her admirable qualities notwithstanding, Enid was made of flesh and blood and therefore subject to the laws and limitations that define all human beings. She could not see into the future nor unravel the mysteries of the past. She was sometimes deceived by appearances. She, too, could make mistakes.

Although Enid was the Queen's most trusted friend, she knew nothing of Guenevere's guilty passion. For Guenevere loved Enid far too well to compromise her integrity in any way. In fact, the Queen took such pains to be discreet that, though Enid was often in the lovers' company, she never suspected a thing. And being free of suspicion herself, she could not guess the reason for Geraint's unhappiness. Nor would Geraint enlighten his wife, for if she were *not* aware of the conspiracy, the very last thing he desired was to put the idea in her mind.

The Prince was determined not to speak. And so, though Enid questioned him repeatedly, for he was often about the castle and thus she had much opportunity to observe his misery, he repeatedly denied that anything was wrong. This made Enid wretched indeed, for unless she understood the nature of his injury, she knew she was powerless to affect any cure. Moreover, if the problem were not attended to, it would only get worse, she feared. Nevertheless, being a dutiful wife,

Enid kept as silent as the Prince and, for his sake, made a noble effort to preserve appearances.

The dramatic change in the Prince's disposition could hardly be expected to go unnoticed at court, however, and Enid soon learned that her husband had become the object of everyone's concern. It saddened her to think that things had come to such a pass. On the other hand, it meant she might approach one or two of Geraint's comrades—Sir Lionel, for example, or Sir Bors perhaps—and try to learn from them the cause of the Prince's wretchedness.

It was a daring plan. For were Geraint to get wind of it, he would surely feel she had betrayed him. Nor would his faith in her be easily restored. Still, fearful lest some accident befall the Prince in his distracted state, Enid decided it was a risk that she must take.

But this proved easier said than done. Enid sensed that Geraint was watching her, and because his movements had lately become so unpredictable, she dared not confer privately with anyone, much less those most likely to benefit her cause. In desperation, she sought the Queen's assistance. And Guenevere arranged that Enid should meet with Sir Lionel, as if by chance, before too many days had been allowed to pass.

❧

Geraint was to have gone hunting in the forest of Broceliande, or at least that is what he told Enid. Whether this was truly his intention remains a mystery; maybe he really did intend to go hunting and then later changed his mind. In any case, he dismissed his page before reaching the wood and, galloping back the way he'd come, arrived within sight of the castle just in time to see Enid and the Queen ride out of the gate.

The ladies were in the habit of riding together frequently, so there was nothing unusual in their doing so that day. They were escorted by several squires and ladies-in-waiting—the customary royal retinue. It was, to be sure, an impressive sight, for the ladies were elegantly dressed—as they were for every occasion—and were mounted on high-spirited palfreys, gorgeous creatures with necks like swans and long, silken manes rippling in the breeze. Still, the sight was an ordinary, everyday sort of thing, such as the Prince had often witnessed with great pleasure in the past. Now, however, spying the party from atop a nearby ridge, the blood turned to fire in his veins.

Spurring on his weary horse the Prince followed them at a safe distance until the party halted beside a lake some leagues from the castle. A moment later, a mounted knight appeared on the opposite bank, and after hailing the ladies, made his way toward the spot where their horses were standing.

From his hiding place behind a stand of pines, Geraint watched the knight approach, then rein in before the ladies and bow in formal greeting. Though he was too far away to overhear their conversation, the Prince was near enough to see the emblem displayed upon the knight's shield and thus to recognize Sir Lionel, his friend of many years.

"Surely my eyes deceive me!" he said to himself.

But, looking again, he clearly perceived the shield with its red lion rampant on a white field: Lionel's insignia.

"What can he be doing here?" Geraint wondered.

Anyone else might have dismissed the knight's presence as mere coincidence. But this possibility never occurred to the Prince. He had no doubt the rendezvous was deliberate, though at first he could not guess its significance. Then it struck him: Sir Lionel was as close a friend to him as Sir Lancelot was to the King!

"God's mercy!" he cried aloud. Seizing the hilt of his sword, he was about to charge down the slope and fall upon Sir Lionel as upon some mortal enemy when another idea came to him and, fortunately, arrested his murderous impulse.

"This must be the Queen's doing!" he raged.

Suddenly it all made sense: Guenevere wished to destroy Enid's innocence, which was obviously a source of shame to the Queen. Moreover, Enid would not dream of betraying the Queen's secret if she were guilty of the same thing. It was a devilish strategy! Still, he had suspected something like this would happen, suspected it from the very beginning. . . .

Meanwhile, Enid returned the knight's greeting and thanked him warmly for his courteous response to her request.

"I only pray I may prove worthy of your confidence," Lionel said.

The knight spoke in all sincerity. For, besides admiring Enid, he was indeed truly a friend and ally of her lord's. Nor was he surprised, therefore, to learn of the anxieties Enid was suffering on Geraint's behalf.

"Though the Prince's behavior of late has inspired the concern of his friends, the cause of his condition remains, alas, a mystery," Sir Lionel sadly confessed. "But," he continued hastily, "do not despair. Whatever is troubling him is sure to pass. Yet I agree it is not seemly for his mind to be turning always inward upon itself. The best remedy would be for him to engage in other things, and to this end, good lady, you may rely on me, for I swear that from this day forth, I shall devote myself to his recovery."

Enid, having pinned all her hopes on Sir Lionel, was grieved to hear him confess his ignorance as to the cause of Geraint's distress. But, fortunately, the knight had been quick to give what sounded like good advice, and this, along with his gallant offer of help, did much to restore her confidence.

Guenevere was a great help to her as well. The Queen hardly spoke, it is true, but only because she had no need to. Her presence was enough. For Guenevere was a Queen in the truest sense, not merely because she was married to Arthur.

She herself was of royal blood, born to be a Queen, and she always conducted herself accordingly.

The following day, Geraint appeared before the King and formally requested permission to leave Camelot. Nor would he say when he might return.

So astonishing was this request that at first Arthur tried to laugh it off—though to tell the truth, its wit escaped him. Then, looking into Geraint's eyes, the King realized his mistake, for he saw that something was seriously wrong. Whereupon the sound of his laughter seemed to fall out of the air and shatter into pieces on the marble floor.

After a moment, Arthur asked to know the reason for Geraint's petition, adding, "Your absence will be grievous to me and can be suffered only on the grounds of absolute necessity."

Geraint hated the idea of lying to the King. It violated all his principles; it was a sin. God would surely punish him. Still, Geraint felt he had no choice; for he dreaded to think about what other, more terrible sins he might commit were he to remain much longer at court. Since the previous day, his mind had been filled with murderous thoughts. Besides, his own fate was secondary. He had to leave Camelot for Enid's sake. He now believed that only by taking her away could he prevent her from being unfaithful to him—and that would be a sin far worse than any *he* might commit.

And so Geraint spoke falsely to the King. "Sire, grave tidings have this day reached me from my own domains, tidings that necessitate my going hence without delay."

Arthur said he was sorry to hear it, then inquired as to the nature of the tidings Geraint had received.

"Close to Devon's northern border lies a wild territory," explained Geraint. "Herein the numbers of lawless elements —bandits, assassins, renegades from the hand of justice and other enemies of the law—have so multiplied of late as to threaten the peace and security of my domain. Therefore, until Your Majesty sees fit to cleanse this vile sewer by force of arms, it is my princely duty to defend the threatened border of my land."

When Geraint had finished speaking, Arthur was silent for a time. The explanation was reasonable, to be sure. Arthur was familiar with the territory Geraint had referred to, and he knew it could well become a refuge for such elements as the Prince had described. Moreover, after several years of peace, there were signs of trouble brewing once again in Arthur's realm. Violence and a growing disrespect for the law were on the rise, especially in the north, according to recent reports. But the King had no idea that the wave of lawlessness had spread so far. If what Geraint said were true, it would surely be cause for alarm. And if Geraint said it, it *must* be true—how could it be otherwise? Unless, of course, the Prince had been misled by false reports. Such mistakes were bound to happen from time to time. Arthur wanted to believe that something of the sort had happened this time. But grave doubts remained in his mind.

Suddenly the King felt tired and sad, burdened by responsibility, disappointed in humanity. For, deep in his heart, he knew Geraint had lied. Nevertheless, out of respect for the Prince, and also because he sensed it would be useless to interfere with his purpose—however ill conceived it might be—Arthur granted Geraint's request.

Geraint thanked him with due courtesy.

Then the King asked when Geraint planned to depart. And upon being informed of the Prince's intention to leave the very next day at dawn, Arthur could not suppress his astonishment. "But why must you leave in such haste?" he cried.

"Sire, the tidings I received were so grave that I have little choice," was Geraint's insincere response.

The King, narrowing his eyes, said, "In that case, I shall be especially anxious to receive news from you."

"So you shall, Sire, upon my word," replied the knight.

After wishing Geraint Godspeed on his journey, the King charged him to return to court as soon as possible. So saying, Arthur sadly concluded the interview.

※

Before the next day had even dawned, Enid and Geraint departed from Camelot. No one bid them good-bye. Except for the guards on duty at the gate, no one saw them go. Hardly anyone even knew they were leaving. They rode off alone, quickly and in silence; like thieves, thought Enid, escaping into the night.

Enid was heartsick. She not only felt grief at their leaving but also was pained by the discourteous way in which Geraint had informed her, the night before, that they were to depart for Devon at dawn. Not that she had any right to criticize Geraint, of course. Still, his refusal to give an explanation for their going had been most ungracious.

"Pray, do not trouble me with idle questions! I shall explain in good time," was all he had said.

The remark had cut her to the quick. Indeed, her first impulse had been to rebuke her husband for his incivility. (Idle questions, indeed!) But, fortunately, she had restrained herself. It was unseemly for a wife to rebuke her husband and could only have made matters worse.

Having galloped at breakneck speed across the still-green meadows—for, though winter was not far off, the first frost had yet to come—Geraint turned onto a narrow trail leading into the hills. Now he was obliged to proceed more moderately. Enid was grateful for this; weak from weeping and lack of sleep, she had reached the limits of her strength.

The opposite was true of Geraint. His spirits had lifted the moment they passed through the castle gate, and they continued to rise with every league he put between himself and the place he believed to be the source of all his suffering.

Presently he remembered Enid, somewhere behind him on the winding trail. Reining in his horse, he waited for her to draw abreast of him. Then, because he regretted his harshness of the night before, he inquired after her welfare with the sincerest courtesy.

Much moved, Enid thanked him for his kindness and replied, "My Lord, as we two are so entwined, such an improvement as I now perceive in your well-being must, of necessity, be reflected in mine."

So fine a sentiment could not but please the Prince exceedingly. Looking about him, he realized that the sky was becoming bright; a mist of pale gold and violet light hung above the far horizon. All of a sudden, Geraint felt as he imagined a sailor might after riding out a storm at sea. His ship wasn't wrecked after all—Enid was devoted to him.

He had not been deceived!

It was as fair a dawn as he had ever seen—a sure sign from heaven that he was right to leave. Of course, Enid might well have remained true to him even had he stayed. But, thanks to his vigilance, she had been spared the test, had been rescued from the Queen's evil influence. He expected no credit for the deed, mind you. Protecting Enid was his sacred duty; her comfort was the only reward he sought.

He thought, "After all, did I not once rescue not only her but her entire *family* from poverty, danger, and despair? I faced death for her then, God knows. And I would do so again, I swear."

Much inspired, Geraint closed his eyes and silently vowed to make any sacrifice—his honor, his life—in the interests of his wife's welfare.

Then, opening his eyes, he beheld a glorious sight: the sun was beginning to rise! Another heavenly affirmation, he decided. Everything was going to be all right—no, *perfect*—from that time forth.

II.

Geraint's gallant rescue of Enid and her family from poverty, danger, and despair is a tale in itself worthy of being told.

It had happened the previous year when, according to custom, King Arthur was holding court at Caerleon upon the river Usk. As usual, the King had taken advantage of the occasion to stage a great hunt, for the lush woods on both sides of the river were filled with deer, wild boar, and many other varieties of game.

On the eve of the hunt, however, Sir Geraint's horse had stumbled and had suffered a minor injury to one leg. The hurt was so slight it doubtless could have been ignored without peril. Nevertheless, the Prince decided not to put on his hunter's green that day. Instead he dressed in a dashing costume of soft leather and gold-threaded silk, and bearing neither sword nor spear, he rode toward a distant knoll from which the hunt could best be seen.

Thereupon he met the Queen, accompanied by a single maid. Clad in rippling purple silks, Guenevere (having dreamed all night of Lancelot) was looking especially lovely. Her hair was as molten gold in the sun, and her face, like a flawless gem, seemed lit by a fire from within.

Delighted by the appearance of Devon's dashing Prince, the Queen returned his compliments, and finding their purposes to be the same, requested the honor of his company.

The two had not been waiting long when a strange sight caught their eye—a knight, a lady, and a dwarf parading by. At the head of the procession rode the knight, his visor raised to show a youthful yet proud and imperious face. Next came the lady, very elaborately dressed and displaying an almost equal haughtiness. And last, but with a manner no less arrogant, rode the dwarf, easily the least appealing figure of the three.

Unable to recall ever having seen the knight in her husband's hall, Guenevere dispatched her maid to inquire his name of the dwarf. But the dwarf, who was of a vicious temperament, rudely declined that she should know it.

"Then I shall ask him myself," said the maid.

"Oh, no you won't!" cried the dwarf. "You are not worthy even to speak to him." And seeing her turn toward the knight, he struck at her with his whip.

Full of indignation, the maiden returned to the Queen. Whereupon Geraint exclaimed, "Surely *I* shall learn his name!" And, making fast for the dwarf, demanded it of him. But the dwarf answered as before, and when Geraint turned toward the knight, the dwarf struck again with his whip, cutting Geraint's cheek so that the blood spurted forth and left a crimson stain upon his sleeve.

Furious, Geraint grasped the hilt of a small dagger—his only weapon—and seemed on the point of annihilating the wretch then and there. But, from exceeding manliness and pure nobility, the Prince restrained his deadly impulse and, saying not a word, turned his horse and rode away.

Regaining the hilltop, Geraint vowed to avenge the insult done upon her maid's person to the Queen, saying, "I shall pursue these vermin to their nest, for though I ride unarmed, surely I shall find someone nearby who is willing to furnish me with the necessary provisions. Then I shall fight this ill-bred knight. I shall force his face into the dust and break his pride—or die myself in the attempt."

The Queen replied, "Farewell, fair Prince. Be successful in this journey as in all your quests. I pray not only for your life but that you may live to wed the one you love. And whether she be the daughter of a beggar or a king, bring her to me on your wedding day, and I shall clothe her in splendor like the very sun."

This promise meant much to the Prince, who was hard-pressed to express his gratitude before hurrying away to make good his pledge.

Through the wooded countryside the Prince pursued his quarry to their destination: a town that bordered a stream running along the bottom of a narrow valley whose fertile slopes were covered with vineyards and fruit-bearing trees. Looking down at the scene, Geraint perceived a newly built fortress on one side of the town and, on the other, a castle crumbling into decay. He saw the knight, the lady, and the dwarf parade slowly through the town to the fortress, then turn into the gate and disappear from sight.

Riding into the town, Geraint had little doubt of finding the provisions he required there. Everywhere he looked men were forging armor: hammering great metal breastplates; repairing coats of mail; and polishing helmets, swords, battle-axes, and other gruesome instruments of war.

The great commotion was on account of a tournament to be held on the following day, and though the Prince pursued his quest for arms with all possible diligence, his efforts were in vain. Moreover, trying to learn the reason for all the preparations proved a vexing task, for every man the Prince approached was rude and churlish, refusing to answer him at

all, or else replying with a single word—"Sparrow-hawk!"
—spoken angrily as though it were a curse.

"Blast this infernal Sparrow-hawk!" cried the Prince,
driven to the end of his patience at long last. "May a thousand
tits eat up your wretched Sparrow-hawk!"

Turning from his forge, the man thus addressed—he was
an old man, stooped and thin—glanced around to make sure
no one was within hearing before he muttered, "Aye, and a
thousand pips peck him to death!"

More than that, however, the man could not be prevailed
upon to say.

By and by, as the sun was starting to set, Geraint sought
food and lodging for the night. But since the town was over-
crowded—visiting merchants and men at arms thronged the
narrow thoroughfare—he met with failure at every turn.

Finally, a damsel took pity on his plight and suggested he
seek shelter at the castle. True, the place had once seen better
days, she said, but the old Duke and his family were known
for their hospitality.

As to this, the Prince was more than a little skeptical.
Nevertheless, being cold and hungry and badly in need of
rest, he felt he had no choice but to proceed to the castle
forthwith.

※

That the place had once seen better days was by no means
an exaggeration. The castle was in a ruinous state, not far

from total collapse. Thick vines obscured the crumbling walls, and thistles sprouted from broken stones in the courtyard. The better part of the tower had fallen in and lay in a great, moss-covered heap upon the ground. Everywhere nature was reasserting her dominion: weeds carpeted the eroding stairs, and ferns grew out of the shattered masonry where once an arched portal must have framed the entrance to the castle's main hall.

Geraint was sorely disappointed by his first impression of the place, but he was not to remain so for long. For the damsel had not misled him as to the old Duke's hospitality any more than she had as to the condition of his residence. In fact, she had likewise understated the case.

Having no servants in his employ, Duke Ynoil himself responded to the stranger's call, inviting him to enter and take his ease, whoever he might be. Then, on learning Geraint's identity, the Duke's kind face grew bright with astonishment and joy. Too moved for words, he made a gesture with his arms, as if throwing open the vanished doors. Geraint came forward and knelt down gallantly upon one knee, at which tears sprang to the old man's eyes.

Having accepted the Duke's hospitality, Geraint was being escorted down a cobwebbed corridor when he heard, or thought he heard, the faint sound of someone singing not far off. The sound was both so soft and so unbelievably sweet that he told himself he must, in his weariness, be imagining things.

Consequently his delight was great indeed when, a moment later, the Duke ushered him into a small but cheerful chamber and presented him to two ladies stationed therein.

The ladies turned out to be Ynoil's wife, the Duchess, and their only daughter, Enid. Besides singing so sweetly (even more sweetly, Geraint thought, than the silver-throated thrush at dawn), Enid was by far the fairest maiden the Prince had ever laid eyes upon. He fell madly in love with her at first sight and decided then and there to move heaven and earth, if need be, to win her as his wife.

Despite their impoverished circumstances, for which they made any number of humble apologies, the ladies were deeply honored to receive the Prince. Geraint would hear none of their protestations, declaring the privilege to be entirely his.

The Duke forbade his guest to lift a finger on his own behalf, but insisted that his daughter would fetch food and drink and see to the Prince's horse herself. All of which Enid did willingly, for she was accustomed to performing such menial tasks for her parents. And, truth to tell, she was so overwhelmed with admiration for the Prince that there was nothing she would have hesitated to do for him.

The Prince was equally admiring of his hosts. For though the family had lost all it once possessed—and he suspected the Duke had been a man of considerable wealth—their spirits appeared to have suffered no ill effects. They were generous, cheerful, and easy to be with. Though they treated him with the utmost deference, he never once felt awkward or embarrassed in their company, for he could not detect any hint of flattery or false humility in anything they said or did.

This was so because, unlike most people, the Duke's family was not impressed by the Prince's power, his prestige, great wealth, or the exceeding manliness of his appearance. Their admiration was excited, rather, by Geraint's heroic exploits and valorous deeds, for these, being popular with minstrels and poets, had come to be known throughout the Kingdom.

Not until their noble guest had eaten and drunk his fill did the Duke see fit to question his purpose in coming there. Whereupon Geraint replied with a full and faithful account of the insult inflicted by the knight's dwarf upon her maid's person to the Queen. His purpose, he explained, was to force the knight, on pain of death, to beg the Queen's pardon for his wickedness.

"And he should have done so already, had my quest for arms been successful," declared the Prince. Then he added, "My enemy was last seen riding into yonder fortress. But, though I tried to find out his identity, no one would enlighten me upon this or any other subject I might care to raise. Do you happen to know the knight I refer to, sir, either by reputation or by name?"

"I do," said the Duke sadly. "He is my nephew."

"You are jesting, surely!" cried the Prince, dismayed.

But the Duke was not jesting. "Alas," he sighed. "He is

my long-dead brother's only living son. And—God have mercy on his soul!—a scoundrel if ever there was one."

Now the Duke's nephew, it appears, had wanted to marry Enid, desperately, for years (which Geraint, of course, was not surprised to hear). But the knight's proposal was not favored by the Duke.

As the old man explained, "My nephew's bad habits are too numerous, his vices too scandalous to name. He is insolent, deceitful, and vain. His ambition, moreover, is unconstrained. He is lustful and he drinks too much. In short, he is not a gentleman, I'm afraid. When I refused him my daughter's hand, he and his men besieged the castle and seized by force of arms my lands, titles, and property. Thus they reduced us to the sorry state you find us in today."

Listening to the Duke, Geraint grew flushed and began breathing rapidly. He was seized by many passions all at once —love, hate, compassion, rage. For a moment, he was so overwhelmed he did not even trust himself to speak.

Perceiving the unsettling effect his words had produced upon the Prince, the Duke leaned forward, patted the Prince's sleeve, and said, "Prince, believe me, I was very foolish in those days. Not that I've changed, of course. But, I know now that I was very much to blame."

Geraint, still speechless, shook his head in disbelief.

But the Duke insisted it was true. "Though I knew him to be untrustworthy, I showed my nephew the hospitality of my hall and allowed him to come and go among us as he pleased. He therefore mingled freely with the men who served me, and by bribes and false promises, he won them to his evil cause. My own means were strained just then—a result of my own foolishness again. And because a flood had caused much hardship in the town, my wicked nephew found it easy to stir the people to rebellion. Alas, many rose against me in the night who once had been my friends."

"For which I pray that God will punish them!" cried the Prince, now more than ever aroused, for such treachery was a truly vile thing to his way of thinking.

The Duke hastened to inform Geraint that everyone now regretted having overthrown him in favor of his nephew, who besides being wicked, was incompetent.

"He is not popular with the inhabitants of this domain," the Duke assured his guest. "In truth, everyone for miles around does nothing but curse his name."

"Soon, God willing, he shall repent his evil deeds," said the Prince. "By the way, what, pray tell, is the scoundrel's name?"

"Out of pure vanity he has renounced the name which was given him and forbids it to be spoken on pain of death," replied the Duke. "He now goes by the boastful title Sparrow-hawk instead."

The name sent a quiver of excitement through the Prince. He was thrilled to hear it. Suddenly it seemed as if all the elements of his life had fallen magically into place. For "Sparrow-hawk" was a name he had already learned to hate.

Now there was no cause for Geraint to feel dismayed, for

he realized that his enemy had done far more mischief to his own family than ever he had done the Queen. Furthermore, he was thrilled to learn that the knight he sought and the wretched Sparrow-hawk were one and the same. Rising from his chair, he eagerly proclaimed his intention to enter the next day's tournament and publicly disgrace his foe—if only his host would furnish him with such arms as were required to achieve this worthy goal.

The Duke did have some arms, and although he said they were in a very sorry state, Geraint was welcome to them. There was another obstacle to Geraint's riding in tomorrow's games, however. No knight could enter his nephew's tournament unless the lady he loved best was also there. The Prince, having no lady with him, would not be eligible.

Glancing about, Geraint was relieved to see that the ladies had withdrawn during the men's long discourse. Whereupon he turned to his host and passionately begged to be allowed to fight in Enid's name, saying he would rather die than bring disgrace on her or her family. If, however, he survived, he would, with the Duke's consent, make Enid his wife, for she was the fairest maiden he had ever seen.

The Duke was much impressed with this declaration. But, he said, his daughter possessed nothing in the way of wealth: no lands, no title, no dowry of any kind.

This meant less than nothing to the Prince. For he said, "Enid is a treasure in and of herself."

When Geraint's enemy was next seen, he was armed from head to toe in black mail, accompanied by fifty squires all waving black banners painted with scarlet sparrow hawks, and mounted on a stallion black as pitch, whose evil disposition went hand in glove with his.

The Duke's nephew, by the way, cared nothing for the haughty lady whose token he displayed. True, he had promised to marry her someday—for the lady, whose pride was surpassed only by her foolishness, desired this above all things —but he had no intention of honoring his pledge. He was still determined to marry his cousin, Enid. It was not that he really loved his cousin—he really loved only himself—but she was the one thing he had ever wanted that he could not seem to get.

Geraint had no one to attend him. Displaying no heraldry, he galloped onto the field, and though the armor he wore was indeed in a sorry state, a hush fell over the assembly the moment he appeared. For the Prince of Devon gave off power as fire gives off heat.

Although the Duke's nephew was a man of little merit, he did have the wit to know trouble when he saw it. On seeing the Prince, he felt a little sick. But then he saw something else—Enid's ribbon flying from the Prince's sleeve, whereupon he was consumed with rage.

The ribbon, a slender strand of rose-colored silk, was easy

to recognize because it had been cut from the hem of Enid's dress—the dress she had been wearing when she and Geraint first met, and which even now she was to be seen in, for it was, alas, the only garment she possessed. Ashamed of her unworthiness yet overwhelmed with joy, Enid had that morning tied the ribbon to the Prince's sleeve, and by so doing had agreed to be his bride.

Now, seeing him gallop onto the field, Enid prayed that her lover would be victorious. What is more, she swore she would be faithful to him forever, whether he lived or died.

The knights took their positions at either end of the field; then, after a fanfare of trumpets, they commenced to charge. Their stallions lunged forward, slowly at first, but quickly gathering speed, making such an awesome, thundering sound that Enid half expected the earth itself to heave and fall away beneath their feet. A moment later, the knights collided with such a fearful clash that every single bird in the valley started into the air.

Geraint easily overthrew his enemy and lost no time in forcing his face into the dust, just as he had promised. Whereupon everyone expressed great joy. They jumped up and down, waving pennants and handkerchiefs, crying death to their fallen lord and long life to the knight who had vanquished him.

When the commotion had subsided, Geraint obliged his victim to turn over, planted a foot on his breast, and commanded him to identify himself.

"I am Edryn, son of Nudd," the fallen knight confessed.

Following more cheers and applause, the crowd began clamoring for Edryn's blood.

Instead of killing his foe, Geraint demanded the following: Edryn, his damsel, and his dwarf should hasten at once to Arthur's court and there crave pardon for their insult to the Queen. And they must agree to abide by the Queen's judgment, whatsoever that might be. Moreover, Edryn had to return to his uncle all that he had stolen from him—his lands, titles, revenues, and all such property as belonged to him by law. If the knight would agree to these terms, he could live; otherwise, Geraint advised him to beg God's mercy on his soul, for he would surely die forthwith.

Edryn agreed reluctantly.

Thus did Geraint rescue Enid and her family from the wretched conditions in which they had long been condemned to live.

※

That night, alone in her bedroom for the last time, Enid sat by the window and watched the crescent moon move slowly through the star-studded sky. Like the moon, she felt as if she, too, had sailed across eternity in a single day. The very shape of her life had changed. How strange and singular it made her feel, almost as if she had been marked for a special fate. And yet her happiness was not complete. That is why, despite the lateness of the hour, she was watching the moon: she could not sleep.

Enid was thinking about what she would wear the following day when the Prince escorted her to Arthur's court. In truth there was only one thing she could wear—her dress of faded rose-colored silk—the dress she had been wearing day in and day out ever since the siege, when Edryn's men made off with nearly all they owned and then, returning, set fire to the rest.

"The Prince is so fine and elegant. Surely it must shame him to be seen with me!" she told herself.

Oh, if only she had one more day! Then, with her mother's help, she could make herself a more presentable dress. But the Prince was in such a rush to be off, and she, being so deeply in his debt, dared not press for a delay. Returning to her bed, Enid slept fitfully.

When the Duchess appeared in Enid's room at dawn, Enid thought she must still be dreaming, for never had she seen such happiness on her mother's face. Then, coming fully awake, she perceived her mother to be holding something— but what? No, she told herself, it couldn't be. And yet, it *was:* a dress of breathtaking beauty!

The dress had been made for Enid long ago, her mother said, but it had been stolen by Edryn's men before it could be given to her.

"And just last night, in secret, it was returned, showing no sign of ever being worn." The Duchess beamed.

But no sooner had Enid risen from her bed when in rushed Duke Ynoil, flustered and out of breath, bearing the most extraordinary message from the Prince.

"Thinking to please him," the Duke said, "I told his lordship all about the dress. Whereupon he, frowning deeply, said, 'Beseech her, please, to put aside her newfound finery in favor of the dress I saw her wearing yesterday.'"

The ladies were astonished at Geraint's request. Nor could they learn the reason for it, since the Prince had not seen fit to volunteer this information. Nevertheless, without further ado, Enid set aside her mother's gift and dressed herself in her worn and faded silks, even as Geraint had bid her to. And though she was most curious to know the reason for his doing so, she made no reference to the matter when, shortly thereafter, she appeared before him once again. Not only did she fear to seem ungrateful, but she also felt too shy to say much of anything to the Prince just then.

The Duchess, however, being equally curious, yet free of all such maidenly constraints, was moved to take the Prince aside and beg him to favor her with an explanation for his odd request. Seizing her two hands in his and calling her Mother for the first time, Geraint informed her of the promise made him by the Queen.

The Duchess, of course, was pleased to hear of Guenevere's generosity. And yet the fact that Geraint had been so secretive she found puzzling indeed.

"I withheld the truth so as to test the force of Enid's love for me," the Prince, his eyes shining, confessed. "I wanted to see if Enid, at my word, would cast aside that which is dear to any woman's heart and must be ten times dearer still to Enid after all her years of suffering and want."

"But her ribbon—she gave it to you as her pledge," the Duchess reminded him.

"Ah, so she did," sighed he, remembering the blissful scene.

"That should have been proof enough for anyone, it seems to me."

"Indeed, it should have been!" exclaimed Geraint. "But because I came upon you all so suddenly, I had my doubts, you see. I feared that, having endured such poverty, Enid might have come to prize the luxuries of court at far more than their worth. And, making some false comparison between herself and me, might argue that I was using her unfairly. Then again, she might have proved more daughter still than wife, caring more for your pleasure than she did for mine. Now I know otherwise. And I shall never doubt her love again as long as we both shall live."

The Duchess held that to be a noble sentiment. She wanted to believe it. But, to risk all for nothing, as Geraint had done, was folly in her opinion. Still, it would not be fitting to say this to the Prince. And since only a fool or a flatterer would say otherwise, she merely smiled at him. Then, seeing how eager he was to be off, she bowed, thanked him for his courtesy, and wished him Godspeed on his journey.

III.

Geraint was greatly relieved to have rescued Enid from Camelot. As soon as they were safely away, his recent suffering came to seem like a dream—fading quickly, in the light of day, into dim memory. Then, too, he was glad to be going to Devon—a place Enid had never seen and that he looked forward with pleasure to showing her. For he wanted nothing more than to devote himself, body and soul, to her welfare.

Late on the day of their leaving Camelot, as they crossed the border into his domain, the Prince thought: "If ever a wife were true to her Lord, so mine shall be to me."

And so, arriving in Devon, Geraint remained day and night in Enid's company and concerned himself with her well-being to the exclusion of all other things.

Thus it came to pass that Geraint forgot his domain and its cares; he forgot the falcon and the hunt, as well as the tilt and tournament. So preoccupied with Enid was he that he forgot about his honor and the glory of his name. And, far worse, he forgot his promise to the King.

As the Prince had now been married for a full year, his excessive devotion to his wife was thought at first to be amusing, and some very funny (but quite indecent) jokes were made at his expense. But the topic of Geraint's love life—spicey though it was—grew stale before too long, whereupon public opinion turned against him. For not surprisingly, people wanted to think of their Prince as being above that sort of thing. It wasn't that he should not be lusty, you understand. On the contrary, a man who was not hot-blooded would hardly be considered a man. Still, to lose oneself entirely to love was a weakness to be frowned upon, especially in someone like the Prince, who was obliged to set an example for the rest—to serve, that is, as a standard of excellence for his subjects.

Thus, news that Geraint had become a slave to love scandalized people. It was a shame and a disgrace. Moreover, it was unmanly—the worst reproach of all.

Enid, who could not help hearing what was said, held herself to blame and so could take no joy in anything. Indeed, far from pleasing her, Geraint's constant attention—his gifts, compliments, and displays of affection—became for Enid a source of guilt and shame. She soon grew weary, too, of constantly pretending to pleasure so as not to offend Geraint. And she was further grieved by the thoughtless comments of her maids—three silly young things who thought to flatter their mistress by forever telling her how fortunate she was to be the object of such devotion and generosity.

It was a dreadful, seemingly endless winter. There came a point, moreover, when Enid could no longer hide her wretchedness from the Prince, who, though obsessed, was not insensitive. And he could not help feeling that all his efforts on Enid's behalf had come to nothing, which made him sad, humiliated, and, alas, increasingly suspicious as to the cause of her misery. For Enid at first would not confess that anything was amiss, much less tell him why she was distressed.

In time, however, aware that the Prince's affairs were in a dreadful state and that if not attended to, they would surely deteriorate, Enid told herself it was her duty to intervene. She must tell the Prince what was being said of him before it was too late. But how she might bring herself to do it—to speak of his shame to his face—she could not begin to see. Indeed, she could not bring herself to *imagine* doing such a dreadful thing! It was like trying to grasp hold of something hot: her mind recoiled instinctively.

"His love for me shall be destroyed," she thought. "And my own life will not be worth living henceforth."

Nevertheless, she dared not postpone the dreadful task of enlightening Geraint.

※

The end of winter was at hand. After a week of dismal weather, there had been a shift in the wind during the night. When dawn finally came, it seemed to Enid as though the sky had been washed clean and hung up like a sheet in the sun to dry.

After a while, the Prince, sleeping by her side, grew heated by the morning light and thrust aside the heavy blanket covering him. Whereupon Enid gazed at him in admiration—his glorious shoulders, his heroic chest—and told herself: "No man could be more grandly made than he!"

Then, all at once, she recalled the awful deed she must perform, and weak from worry and lack of sleep, she fell to weeping over Geraint.

Was it true, as people said, that all the Prince's force was spent? Could it be that he had lost his manhood and become effeminate? If so, was she to blame for the catastrophe? Such questions had been tormenting Enid for weeks. Now, though they troubled her as much as ever, she knew they did not matter. She had to repeat the accusations to Geraint today, before it was too late.

"I have been wrong to let him linger on in ignorance so long!" she told herself, and so saying, fell into another fit of grief.

"Alas!" she cried out a moment later. "To think that he should suffer such shame through me. Would I had never been born than live to cause such suffering and pain. And better to be dead than to know his love will never shine on me again."

Once more her body shook with sobs. Then, when the storm had passed, she reproached herself for being weak and selfish.

"What wickedness to put my loss before my lord's!" she

declared. "How if he suffered not only shame but also injury —or even death—through my neglect? O God, forgive my sinfulness, I pray! For I have been a faithless wife to Geraint!"

Because she was beside herself, Enid spoke these words aloud while continuing to shed bitter tears—some of which fell upon her husband's naked breast and caused him to awaken even as she was nearing the end of her lament. Thus he overheard only the latter fragment of her words—the part, that is, about her sinfulness and how she had been a faithless wife to him.

His worst fear had come to pass! He thought: "Despite my pains, she is untrue—faithless by her own report. All this time she has been pining for some knight in Arthur's hall!"

Geraint then bestirred himself with sudden violence. Heaving his body from the bed, he summoned his squire with such force you might have thought the boy was sleeping clear across the courtyard instead of right outside their chamber door.

The lad entered directly, tugging at his rumpled tunic.

"Make ready my charger and her palfrey!" Geraint cried.

Then, as the lad hesitated (in case there might be something more), the Prince spoke harshly to him, as if rebuking him from some gross negligence, ordering him to look smart and do as he was told. Flushing crimson, the squire went rushing from the room.

The Prince turned to Enid and with equal vehemence said, "Go, put on your worst, your plainest dress. We journey forth at once—into the wilderness!"

Enid did not realize her inward thoughts had been audibly expressed, and so she was filled with astonishment. "If I have committed some offense, pray tell me what it is," she begged.

But he, fearing to be beguiled by her charms, exclaimed: "Speak not, I charge you, but *obey*!"

The old rose-colored dress lay buried in a cedar chest with sprigs of flowers in among the folds. Enid took it up and paused, recalling the time Geraint first came upon her wearing it, and all her foolish fears about the dress, and how the Prince had loved her then. After which, she made haste to do as she had been told.

Having done so, she turned to behold her sorry image in the glass, and thought: "Through my own fault the very thing I feared has come to pass. I should have spoken long ago. . . . Now all is lost."

Geraint could not bear the sight of Enid in the dress whose history he recalled, of course, with equal vividness. And so, when they had mounted their horses, he said, "Ride not by my side. Rather, go before, and make sure to keep a fair distance between us. And remember: not a word to me! Speak, for whatever reason, and you cease to be my wife in all but name."

This punishment was cruel indeed. Yet, because Enid's

remorse was so great, it seemed to her somehow fitting. Thus she did not hesitate but spurred her horse and rode off without daring so much as a backward glance at Geraint.

Watching her go, it seemed to the Prince that she had been only too willing to get away.

"Since she has another lover, my presence must be hateful to her," he reasoned. The thought caused him great pain, you may be sure. But then another, far more painful thought occurred to him. "Why then, my presence must have been hateful to her all along!"

Suddenly, he remembered how, for months now, he had been forcing himself upon his wife, encompassing her with sweet observances and passionate caresses at all hours of the day and night. Whereupon, in his agony reason left him, and he despised himself and every living thing.

※

With Enid in the lead, the two rode swiftly. By noon they had crossed Devon's northern border.

Now, Geraint had secured King Arthur's permission to leave Camelot the previous fall because he had falsely asserted that his domain was threatened by lawless elements from the north. In fact, there had been a rumor of lawlessness, but having come from an unreliable source, the Prince had not considered it credible. And because he had so regretted the sin of lying to his sovereign, Geraint had willed himself to forget the incident and everything connected with it.

Heedless of his promise to the King, Geraint had failed to inquire into the true state of things in the wild territory. Had he done so, he would have been surprised to find that he had not lied to Arthur after all. For though the situation was not as grim as he had pretended to suspect, it was, even then, a cause for alarm. Moreover, having been so long unchecked, the lawless elements had flourished and spread. Now they presented a threat every bit as great as Geraint had originally alleged.

The wilderness was a hideous place—a marshy waste of tangled roots and nettles, spiny bushes, briars, and strangling vines. From the mangled branches of half-dead trees hung a hairy netting of moss and ferns so thick that though the sun might be directly overhead, the atmosphere within was forever dark, dank, and deathly still. Vapors rising from numerous stagnant pools permeated the air with a noxious smell. Neither bird nor any beast that man is pleased to look upon ventured near the region, which instead teemed with the vilest things—bats, vipers, and the like, creatures that thrive in darkness and are loathsome to men's sight. And little better than the beasts were the desperate men who dwelled therein, for none but hardened criminals and lunatics dared enter that godforsaken realm.

Why the Prince decided to travel through so inhospitable a neighborhood, Enid was at a loss to explain. Even Geraint, once in the wilderness, realized he had made a mistake. He should have taken a more direct route to his destination, that being the town in which he had first found Enid and where he intended to return her, like a piece of damaged property, to her father's hall. At the peak of his rage, however, he had made up his mind to travel there by the meanest route so as to cause her the greatest suffering.

Now that his passion had cooled, the Prince regretted his decision. He considered changing his plan, ordering Enid about and hurrying back with her across the border. For a moment he even imagined opening his heart to her. But, alas, it was impossible. What could he say? He could sooner strike her dead than accuse her of infidelity. And so he rode onward as before.

Meanwhile, Enid, riding ahead of her husband, had come upon three bandits. Perceiving her to be alone, the villains swaggered forth from their bandit-hold, intending to lay hands upon her person.

Before they could do so, Geraint appeared in the distance. The three rogues halted, and taking council among themselves, decided to fall upon him unaware and slay him for his horse and armor. As soon as they hid themselves, however, Enid hastened back along the trail to warn Geraint of the conspiracy.

Geraint, vexed at her for disobeying his command, and thinking the warning an insult to his manhood, scorned her courtesies and admonished her to speak no more to him.

Then, telling her to stand aside, he drew his sword, dug his spurs into his stallion's flanks, and charged into the midst of his enemies.

One of the scoundrels was fortunate: he died instantly. The other two took somewhat longer to expire and underwent much agony. Enid pitied them, although she knew they had inflicted similar fates on countless innocent wayfarers in their day.

Further on, Enid encountered an even larger band of outlaws, and finding their purpose to be like that of the first, she again felt compelled to retrace her steps and make Geraint aware of the danger to his welfare. His response was true to form, save that on this occasion his outrage was so great that he charged his wife, upon her very life, to speak no more to him. Then, forcing her startled horse into the shrubbery, he galloped off and laid waste his enemies.

The two rode on for some time without suffering further abuse. But then, nearing the end of the trail, Enid beheld a large gathering of armed and evil-looking men in a clearing. Having no doubt as to their intentions, she resolved to wait there and forewarn Geraint of the peril ahead.

"My lord is weary from his previous encounters," she reasoned. "Falling upon him unaware, these villains are likely to succeed where the others failed."

True, she had been charged on her life to keep silent. But that deterred her not at all. "If he kills me, so be it," she thought.

Geraint, downcast and beleaguered, appeared a minute later. Nor did he become aware of Enid until she hailed him from a few paces away.

She asked his leave to speak.

"You take it by speaking," he said.

And she informed him of the intended ambush, adding apologetically that several of the assassins appeared, from a distance at least, to be nearly as large of limb as he.

"Were there a thousand villains all twice my size they would not cause me half so much distress as does your disobedience!" he replied hotly.

Geraint disapproved of disobedience in anyone. But he could more readily accept it in a man. Men were by nature argumentative, whereas ladies were naturally inclined to be submissive. Therefore, when a lady disobeyed authority, she did violence to her true nature, and this was an insult to God, her creator. Or in other words, a sin. Such, at any rate, was Geraint's opinion.

Had Enid disagreed with him, she might have been spared much pain. But her views, alas, were similar to his. This being so, her heart and mind were not united. Indeed, she was on the point of throwing herself at the Prince's feet and begging him to put an end to her misery when he ordered her to stand aside and once again charged ahead, sword in hand.

The Prince's rage served him well. In the battle that followed, he succeeded in annihilating every man who raised a sword against him. Nevertheless, in the course of the massacre he sustained an injury that, although not apparent to the eye, was very grave.

Now the Prince was like a traveler in some distant land to whom a dreadful loss has happened of which he is unaware. But then, upon returning home, he learns of it and, overwhelmed by grief, sickens to the point of death.

Thus fared it with Geraint. Stabbed in the heat of combat and bleeding secretly beneath his armor, he managed for a time to make little of his injury. Even when the pain became too great to be denied, he rode on in stony silence, concealing every outward sign of his distress. But at last the pain of the wound swelling within his metal breastplate became intolerable. By then he had lost a prodigious amount of blood. His limbs were cold as ice, his mouth dry as a sun-scorched stone. As his horse rounded a turn in the road he was seized with dizziness. He heard his voice cry out as if from a great distance. Then, suddenly, there was a great, roaring sound as the world slid out from under him. . . .

❧

A moment after she saw him fall, Enid was beside Geraint's seemingly lifeless form, clawing at the blood-soaked fastenings of his armor. But they held fast, despite her desperate efforts. She seized the Prince's dagger, and uttering small, grief-stricken cries, slashed through the bonds and removed the armored plate. Whereupon, seeing the Prince drenched in his own blood, Enid screamed. For a moment, hysteria nearly overwhelmed her, but she fought it back, and used the blade to slit open the front of Geraint's bloody tunic. Whereupon, she screamed again, but this time in relief, and cried, "Heaven be praised—he breathes!"

Then she saw, to her horror, fresh blood surging forth from the Prince's wound. Any breath could be his last, she realized, and so she proceeded to tear from the skirts of her dress several strips of silk, which she bound tightly about the Prince's breast. The flow of blood thus staunched, she threw off her cloak and spread it over him, and with her veil wiped the sweat and dirt from his face. After which, having done all that was humanly possible, she sank to her knees and prayed for God to send someone to her aid.

Time passed, the crimson sun was setting, yet no one came. Enid's desperation turned to despair, for she had little hope of finding anyone abroad in that lonely region once night fell. But just when she thought the end was at hand, she heard men's voices. A moment passed, then out of the dusk five armed knights came riding toward her.

Rising unsteadily to her feet, Enid hailed the strangers. Gesturing to Geraint, she said, "Kind sirs, have pity on this noble knight, who lately was attacked by vicious outlaws, all of whom fell victim to his sword. However, he too, was wounded in the fray. And so, I pray you, bear him from here, for unless he's given shelter for the night, he shall not live to see the light again, except it be the light of heaven."

Bareheaded and wearing blood-splattered rags, Enid was an arresting sight. The riders stopped, struck by her fearful beauty, and stared.

She waited, eyes downcast, trembling. Then, to her great amazement, she heard someone shout her name. She looked up. A rider leaped from his horse and came rushing toward her, arms outstretched. Suddenly, she recognized her cousin Edryn!

"Heaven save me," she sighed, then fainted dead away.

※

"Enid, the only ray of light in my dark life! My early and my only love. Great is my joy to see you here."

The heat of Edryn's breath in her ear brought Enid to her senses all at once. She found herself lying in a great hall. Shocked, she started to rise, but her cousin restrained her, clutching her arm.

"Oh, Enid, whose loss has turned me wild! Chance has finally put you in my power!" he exclaimed.

The knight's eyes were moist with passion. It was obvious that he had been drinking heavily. Enid felt torn between gratitude and dismay.

Geraint lay beside her, motionless, gray, yet breathing. For which she was thankful to her cousin. However, Edryn's hot breath and the feel of his clammy hand upon her skin were sickening. He was at once the answer to her prayer and, alas, her worst nightmare. She hesitated, therefore, not knowing what to say to him.

"Dear Enid," he said, "you looked upon me favorably once, until your father came between us. In truth I have not known a moment's happiness between that day and this. Oh, cousin, the love you had for me in former days cannot be dead! Give me reason to hope, to live! You must, for half my life has already been lost through your fault."

Now, though Enid was truly in a wretched state as a result of her recent suffering and long abstinence from food and drink, she was still capable of telling true from false. And the truth was, she had never loved her cousin nor given him the slightest reason to hope that she did. Therefore, she resented being blamed for his life of idleness and sin. For one thing was certain: Edryn had not reformed. Indeed, judging from his fine clothes and the magnificent hall they were in, he was living in great style, despite having long since squandered such wealth as rightfully belonged to him.

Seeing Enid glance about the hall, Edryn smiled and said, "Say you'll make me happy, and all this shall be yours, and more. Nor shall you ever go abroad unattended, dressed as you are now in wretched rags! And yet, it makes me glad to see you thus, for it proves that you are out of favor with your lord. In truth, he's made of you a public mockery. Oh well, so fares it frequently with men, I know. And once his love is gone, never shall you win it back again; for a man's love, once dead, never returns."

These words filled Enid with profound despair. But Edryn dismissed her grief with a wave of his hand.

"Nevermind," he declared. "Though his love is dead, mine lives on. Indeed, my passion now is greater than it's ever been!"

Enid did not doubt it. And well remembering the violence Edryn's passion had inspired in the past, she replied to him with greater craft than honesty, begging him, in the interests of common decency, to leave her yet awhile. For, she said, it was her duty to tend her husband to the end.

Edryn cared not at all for Enid's duty, and even less for common decency. Nevertheless, calculating that his purpose would best be served by paying her this courtesy, he withdrew for a time from the hall.

※

Enid remained with Geraint, propping up his head and rubbing his cold hands and feet, kissing, caressing him, and calling out his name. At last he awoke to find her ministering to him.

As he heard her words and felt her tears upon his cheek, he thought, "By heaven, she weeps for me." Yet no sign did he make, but lay still, as if upon the point of death, in order to put Enid's love to the utmost test.

Meanwhile, Edryn had repaired to the banquet hall where he passed the time drinking and boasting of his latest conquest. Presently, accompanied by a band of less than sober lords and ladies, he staggered back along the corridor to claim, once and for all, the one thing that had eluded him for so long.

But when he entered the hall, he saw Enid still weeping her heart out over Geraint. Enraged, he shouted, "God's curse— it makes me mad to see you thus! Come, it is enough. Alive, your husband scorned your love; his death does not deserve your grief. After all, would he have shed a single tear if you were in his place? Come, therefore," he said, becoming suddenly expansive. "Eat something."

Enid made no move.

Edryn ordered her to rise and leave her place beside Geraint.

But this she would not do.

Vexed, Edryn stormed across the hall and seized his cousin. Then ignoring her cries of protest, he dragged her by force to the serving board. Once there, he threw some meat upon a silver plate and thrust the plate beneath her face, shouting, "Eat, I say!"

Still she refused.

Edryn flung aside the plate; it struck a servant in the head, then fell with a crash to the floor. Upon which, Edryn, suddenly inspired, grasped a skin of wine and cried, "Of course! You'd rather drink!"

Advancing once again, he tried to force the skin on Enid, spilling wine on both of them.

"I should have known!" he said. "Why, I myself can never eat until I've had a drink or two. Here, take it and drink your fill."

But Enid would not hear of it. "No," she cried. "Not one

drop shall pass my lips unless my lord can drink as well. And if he does not rise and bid me drink with him, I'll never look at wine until I die."

Flinging aside the wineskin with a curse, Edryn commenced to pace back and forth, gnawing at his lower lip. Then, drawing close to his cousin, he warned her against scorning any more of his courtesies.

"Yonder lord lies dead," he told her, "and the people here obey my will. I advise you to be reasonable. Consider your own welfare. Remember, your lord cared less for you than for the beast who bore him hither, for his horse is comparisoned in silver, while you in the meanest rags are sent abroad. So weep no more for him. Besides, he can no longer hear you. He is gone."

Panic-stricken, Enid started toward the Prince.

Edryn snatched hold of her sleeve, crying, "Nevermind him, by heaven. Attend to me!"

She tried unsuccessfully to free herself, for she was desperate to find out how it fared with Geraint. But Edryn had no thought for Enid's suffering; all his thoughts were for himself—his disappointment, his disgrace.

"Take heed, cousin," he told her through clenched teeth. "My honor and reputation are at stake."

But she would not take heed. And the more she struggled, the more enraged he became, until it seems he lost not merely his reason but all such qualities as are said to distinguish men from beasts. He struck his cousin—slapped her, *hard,* across the face.

The piercing scream that Enid uttered was not so much inspired by the stinging blow, which brought tears to her eyes and left a scarlet stripe upon her cheek, as by her sudden, horrible conviction that Geraint no longer lived. For Edryn would not have done this dreadful deed, she thought, unless he knew for sure Geraint was dead.

Enid's reasoning made perfect sense, but her conclusion was false, thank heavens, nonetheless.

Geraint, far from dead, had already jumped to his feet, sword in hand. Before anyone knew what was happening, another scream was echoing through the hall, and Edryn, clutching his side, stared in horror as his blood spilled onto the marble floor. . . .

※

"Enid, I have done you far more harm than that man ever did," Geraint said when everyone had fled in panic from the hall—everyone save Edryn, who lay sprawled upon the floor.

Enid was speechless with relief and joy.

"It grieves me so to think how cruelly I have used you," continued the Prince, his voice trembling with remorse. "All I can say is the ordeal I forced you to endure has made me yours ten times over. Never again will I doubt your love, I swear. Nor shall I question you as to the meaning of those words I overheard you say today at dawn—that you were no true wife and had been faithless to me. Though the declaration caused me more suffering than I can say, I'll never ask you to explain it."

Now, more than ever in her life, Enid was at a loss for words. She cast about for a reply in vain. Then, coming to her rescue once again, Edryn groaned aloud. For it seems he was not dead but only gravely wounded.

Surprised, Geraint raised his sword, intending to finish the wretch off once and for all. Whereupon Enid, falling to her knees, beseeched him to spare her cousin's life. Edryn would have a change of heart, she said. Indeed, he would become a different man entirely if only he were allowed to live. Not only would he repent his past misdeeds, but he would devote himself henceforth to Arthur's cause.

Never having heard his wife foretell the future before, Geraint was truly amazed by what she said. And considering how badly she had been used by Edryn, her request made little sense to him. Still, he did not hesitate to honor it, for now he trusted Enid completely.

Finally, he had faith.

"Henceforth I shall let her guide me in all things," he thought, overwhelmed with reverence for his wife.

But this was no time to stand idly by, he suddenly realized! There was thunder in the corridor—Edryn's men, no doubt, returning to avenge his murder! (Edryn, motionless on the floor, appeared every bit as dead at this point as Geraint had heretofore.)

"Come!" cried the Prince, helping Enid to rise. "We must fly!"

But instead of doing so, they fell into a passionate embrace.

Soon, however, perceiving it was now or never, they wrenched themselves apart and started for a likely looking exit at the far end of the hall. If only they could leave the room unseen, they thought they might escape the castle easily.

Nor was this assumption false: the portal gave onto an outer gallery encircled by a wall of no great height. Their horses, moreover, were tethered nearby. They had only to reach the door in time . . . but alas! this proved impossible.

Anxious, no doubt, to forestall just such an escape as Enid and Geraint were attempting, their enemies had proceeded in great haste along the corridor. Before the two could reach their destination, a multitude of men—several dozen at least, judging from the din—burst into the hall behind them.

It was too late!

Too late for Geraint, at any rate. Enid might yet escape if Edryn's followers could be held at bay. And so, happy to die gloriously for Enid's sake, the Prince begged his wife to go on without him. He begged her repeatedly, desperately—but in vain. Enid was deaf to his entreaties.

"So be it, then," Geraint cried out. "Our fate is in God's hands!" Whereupon they turned, expecting to encounter certain death.

But happily, that tragedy was not to be.

Enid and Geraint indeed beheld a multitude of well-armed

knights charging toward them. But the difference between what they anticipated and the sight they actually perceived was like the difference between darkest night and brightest day. For the knights had come, not to murder, but to *rescue* them. They were not enemies! They were Geraint's comrades, Knights of the Round Table, *friends!* Furthermore, King Arthur himself was leading the company.

So astonished was the Prince by the spectacle of Arthur and his fellow knights rushing toward him that his sword literally fell from his grasp. One might have thought he had been struck down after all, except he recovered so quickly—brought to his senses, apparently, by the sound of his blade striking the floor.

After the excitement subsided, the King told Enid and Geraint how he had happened to come upon them.

He and his men were in the neighborhood when they heard tell of much bloodshed nearby. One knight, so the story went, had singlehandedly vanquished a great many desperately wicked men known to have been plaguing the region for some time.

"The exact number of dead was impossible for us to guess," the King said. "For as you would expect, people differed widely in their estimates."

Still, not doubting that much blood had been spilled, Arthur was eager to reward the knight responsible for this service to the Kingdom. A little while later, however, the King's party was informed that the gallant knight had been wounded and lay dying—if not already dead—in a castle some leagues hence.

"These were evil tidings," sighed the King. "Nevertheless, we repaired to the castle without delay. Whereupon, perceiving your charger tethered outside, our astonishment was surpassed only by the great anxiety we suffered on your behalf."

The King's men promptly stormed the halls and ran riot through the corridors, desperately hoping to reach the Prince before he died. And then, what joy they felt at finding Geraint alive and well!

What Arthur did *not* tell Geraint was how he happened to be in the neighborhood in the first place. His being near at hand was not, as he'd implied, an accident. Rather, he and his company of hand-picked men had come to cleanse the wild territory of the evil elements that were infesting it.

Arthur's failure to mention this was more than courteous. For though he had heard countless complaints about the miserable state of things in the region, he had heard nothing, *not one word,* from the Prince. And the Prince, after all, had ridden off months before in order to investigate the area, and, furthermore, had promised to render the King a full report at the earliest opportunity. The King did not refer to these things, however, partly out of regard for the Prince and partly because he knew that doing so would serve no useful purpose.

For Arthur had received complaints from Devon as well, and he was therefore aware that the Prince had been neglectful of his duties. His affairs were in disarray. Apparently, his problem was of a personal nature, but more than that the King neither knew nor cared to discover. Whatever the difficulty might have been, the details did not interest him and were, in his opinion, best forgotten.

As for Enid, she came to adopt a policy similar to the King's, for her wisdom equaled his in many things. But, as Enid's curiosity was so much greater than the King's, her restraint was virtuous in the extreme.

Enid never ceased to wonder why Geraint had suddenly lost faith in her in the first place. Indeed, this question often preyed upon her mind. Nor did she suppose the answer would be hard to come by, for Geraint would not withhold it from her, she was sure, if only she requested it of him.

But she never did.

She did not think it would be wise to disrupt the balance of their lives merely to satisfy her curiosity. Her husband's faith, after all, had been more than restored; he was truly hers ten times over. Though courteous before, he now accorded her such respect as men pay only to other men. Once they returned to Devon, he began regularly to seek her council upon weighty matters—not just privately, in the bedchamber, but in open court. The practice made Enid nervous at first, for it was highly unusual. Furthermore, the responsibility was very great. But things went well from the moment they returned, and got so much better as time went on, that Enid soon set aside her fears and gratefully used her powers for the benefit of all.

And so she never gave in to the temptation to question Geraint.

"Curiosity is an idle child," she decided. "Its wants are indiscriminate and never satisfied." Besides, if the answer had been good for her to know, Geraint would have told it to her long ago.

Nor was Enid mistaken. The Prince would have faithfully replied to her question at any time. Moreover, he was sure the issue would be raised eventually and admired his wife's restraint in not putting the question to him right away. But as weeks became months and she made no reference to the matter, Geraint's admiration for her grew. Though he knew she must be curious to know the cause of all their suffering, he did not volunteer to solve the mystery, for he believed it would be best to dismiss the possibility of the Queen's faithlessness once and for all. Whether the charge be true or false, the Queen's conduct was her own affair. He had his affairs to attend to, affairs he had neglected far too long.

❦

Few believed that Edryn could survive his injury, given his condition and the fact that he soon succumbed to a raging fever and lay, delirious, for many days at death's door. His recovery, therefore, was spoken of with awe, as something heaven must have had a hand in. This notion was supported by the fact that Edryn himself was quite transformed. The fever had scorched clean his soul. Everyone said so.

As soon as he had strength enough to ride, Edryn made his way alone to Camelot where he sought and was granted an audience with the King. Whereupon Edryn begged to be allowed to serve Arthur's sacred cause in any, be it the most humble, capacity. Arthur bid him rise—which Edryn did with difficulty, being thin as a wraith and weak from traveling—and accepted the knight's services with due courtesy.

Edryn soon proved an excellent knight—strong, fearless, reliable—and he always served the King faithfully, even as Enid had foretold.

※

Enid and Geraint did not return to Camelot, save for visits now and then. Instead, with the King's permission, they chose to live out their days in Devon.

There was no necessity for them to do so; the Prince's affairs were soon put in order, and the state again ran smoothly, like a ship before the wind. Nor was Devon threatened from without, for the King's company had ridden forth into the wilderness straightaway and eliminated any evil elements that remained, though most of them had already been dispatched by Geraint.

Then, strange to say, the area itself began to change, and come to life slowly. Animals started to inhabit it again. Flowers grew. Trees bore fruit. Much later, long after King Arthur and his knights were no more, the region became a refuge for wild birds and beasts, some of which would otherwise have been hunted to extinction.

Enid and Geraint were never quite the same following their long ordeal and near escape from tragedy. They retired to Devon, not because they scorned the life at court, but rather because the spectacle of wealth and power had ceased to fascinate them. Excitement and novelty—the daily fare at Camelot—were delights that Enid and Geraint no longer craved.

In any event, as they soon had children—five of them, one right after the other—traveling was no longer a casual affair.

So they remained where they were for the most part, and their lives were much like those of other folk—except that they did things on a somewhat grander scale than most, and knew such joy as people know whose lives and all they love are lost for a time and then, by a miracle, are restored to them.

MERLIN

and

NINIANE

ERLIN, THE CREATOR OF THE ROUND TABLE AND all its splendors, was the greatest magician who ever lived. He was the power behind the King's established order; all the deeds done by Arthur and his knights were guided by the Wizard's hand.

A youth when first he came forth from the forest, Merlin stayed to work his power in the world until he was very old. Whereupon, realizing that all must come to pass as he had foretold, he began to withdraw from Arthur's court and the world of his fame and took to wandering deep in the forest once again.

One morning, while in the woods of Broceliande, the Wizard came upon a beautiful denizen of that enchanted realm, a wild fairy maiden by the name of Niniane, dancing all alone in a clearing.

Being the daughter of Diana, the famous Sicilian siren, Niniane had been endowed with many wondrous charms, all of which were immediately obvious to Merlin. In no time, he was spellbound—bewitched by her eyes that flashed like stars behind the clouds of her shimmering silver hair. And by her body—straight and strong as a young tree (for she was all but naked, naturally)—whirling so freely about the clearing.

In Niniane, the Wizard recognized his destiny: she would be his undoing. And yet the sight of her gave him more pleasure than all the worldly splendors he had ever thought to create. And, in the course of his long life, Merlin had created splendors too numerous to name. Watching Niniane, however, the Wizard forgot his past and all its glories. Before long, he had ceased to be aware that there was even a world beyond the forest. Then he ceased to be aware of the forest. . . .

Niniane was likewise delighted to behold the Wizard—whose appearance was accompanied by flashes of colored lightning and great quantities of rose petals falling out of the clear blue sky. Though such an unexpected and spectacular display would surely have unsettled any ordinary maiden, Niniane went wild with glee. For she, being a fairy-child, had no fear of anything. Besides, she quickly recognized the Wizard's distinctive figure. Whereupon, rushing to his side, she greeted him so warmly that he must have felt deeply gratified even had he been indifferent to her charms. Bewitched as he was, the Wizard kept his calm only with the greatest difficulty. And so, when Niniane begged to see more of his magic arts, Merlin was only too happy to oblige.

Raising his wand, the Wizard drew a circle in the air while murmuring an incantation. Thereupon a company of troubadors materialized out of nowhere, and accompanying themselves on a variety of instruments, began singing more beautifully than it is possible to imagine.

Niniane listened, enraptured, for a long time.

Presently, as the sun had risen to its height, the Magician gave a sign, and a shady arbor unfurled overhead. Nearby, a fountain spurted out of the ground; lush flowers and sweet-smelling herbs sprang up in the grass around them.

Niniane took great delight in each and every thing, and as she was by nature neither devious nor shy, she expressed her admiration freely.

"Ah, would that you could entertain me all the time!" she cried.

Whereupon, Merlin revealed to her the passion that was in his heart. Without hesitating, Niniane replied to him in kind, and what is more, embraced him eagerly.

Although Niniane promised to meet Merlin in the forest the very next day, the Magician felt heartsick as the time neared for him to return to court. And when, just as they were about to part, Niniane clung to him and begged him to teach her the secrets of his magic art, he readily assented. Because he could not, for the life of him, imagine denying her anything just then, or possibly ever again.

※

Merlin was as good as his word. Upon his return, he introduced Niniane to the basic principles of sorcery, then taught her the elements of several simple spells—the one for making rainbows, for example—as well as a charm for curing sundry maladies (including headaches, baldness, stuttering, hiccups, and mild forms of lunacy).

In her delight, Niniane gave ever more freely of herself to the Wizard. And he realized that his desire for her was such as could never be satisfied. Lying on a carpet of moss, concealed by a warm white mist, Merlin and Niniane swore that they would love each other forever. After which, they made joy out of mind and time.

Their parting on this occasion was many times more painful than before, especially for Merlin, who had to return to

Arthur's court, an altogether different world. For though the Magician had removed himself to a great extent from the affairs of men, certain worldly matters still required his attention.

But Merlin came as often as he could to Niniane, and each time she received him more ardently. While they lay enraptured in each other's arms, the Wizard taught her all sorts of singular things; what is more, he endowed her with powers beyond anyone's wildest dreams.

For no teacher, before or since, has ever had a more receptive pupil, nor one with quicker wits or sharper perceptions. Indeed, Niniane could hear a leaf fall; and she saw things—distant stars, for instance—few eyes have ever perceived. Then, too, she had exceedingly nimble fingers; her touch, therefore, was wise and sure. Her memory, even for intricate manipulations and complicated incantations, also was superb. And she had perfect pitch.

Thus it is not surprising that Niniane soon became adept in the art of sorcery. For Merlin could withhold nothing from her and taught her more and more each time they met.

Yet, as their joy in each other increased, so did the pain of their partings. One day, Merlin knew he could bear it no longer and swore that upon his return, he would remain with Niniane in the forest forever.

"I bid you farewell for the final time," he declared. "Henceforth, I shall be always by your side."

So saying, Merlin returned to Camelot where he shut himself up in his spiral tower. Summoning all his powers of concentration, he reviewed everything that had ever happened to him, beginning with the moment of his conception. The process took him three whole days, during which he refrained from eating anything and drank but rarely from a vessel that contained a mysterious, bitter-smelling drink.

Then, having completed his task, Merlin took his leave of Arthur's worldly domain. And no one, not even the King, was to lay eyes upon the Wizard's face again.

※

Disappearing into the ancient forest of Broceliande, Merlin entered a living tapestry woven of every imaginable shade of green. Beneath a vaulted awning of sunlit leaves, the air was cool as water and filled with the scents of plants. Rosemary, lavender, mimosa, pine—Merlin passed through spheres of different fragrances. Like figures in a tapestry, wild animals appeared to him, for none of the forest creatures had any fear of Merlin. On the contrary, a pair of silver foxes often trotted at his side; birds flew out of the treetops to light on his shoulders; does gazed up at him with melting eyes.

Pressing onward, Merlin soon came to the innermost heart of the forest where his fairy-mistress was waiting. She received him more willingly than ever, thereby giving him more pleasure than words can possibly describe. And so, when she begged him to grant her one last favor, he assured her that she need only name her desire for it to be instantly gratified.

And so she said: "Teach me how, without chains or iron bars, I may restrain a man, purely by magic, so he will be powerless to leave me unless I myself shall choose to set him free."

After she had spoken, the Magician stared into the distance, saying nothing for quite some time. Then he sighed and turned to Niniane. Holding nothing back, he taught her the various elements of what was by far his most powerful spell. And Niniane, in her gratitude, embraced him so passionately and gave him so generously of her love that he knew he would never again be happy unless she was beside him.

Merlin knew what was to be. And yet, that day, as he wandered hand in hand with Niniane through the forest of Broceliande, he was not mindful of his destiny. His thoughts were all in the present, with Niniane.

Though she had a woman's form, Niniane was such a wild mixture of inventiveness and whim that she did not seem at all human. To Merlin, who could see through appearances to the True Essence of things, Niniane was a flame, a source of bright, spellbinding energy.

By and by, the Wizard began to grow weary, for he had had no sleep in many days. And so the lovers sat down to rest in the shade of a blossoming whitethorn bush. Here they passed some time kissing and whispering sweet endearments until, overcome by drowsiness, Merlin lay down with his head in Niniane's lap. Niniane sat there, running her fingers through his long white hair, until he slept at last.

When she was certain he was sound asleep, Niniane rose, and letting her long veil trail behind her on the ground, she circled three times around the whitethorn bush while uttering an incantation. Then, stepping inside the magic circle she had inscribed, she walked nine times around the Wizard, nine times around the whitethorn bush, whispered nine times the proper magic words, and thus cast the incredibly powerful spell Merlin had taught her. Then she sat down and once again took the Wizard's head in her lap.

Merlin awoke to find himself surrounded by a high wall, seemingly of stone. Yet, behind the wall he could see, very dimly, the image of the forest. His heart sank, for he recognized at once that he was no longer free. Here, on account of a fairy-maiden's whim, he must remain, perhaps for the rest of eternity.

He prayed Niniane not to betray him. "Say you will be true to your vow and stay with me forever. For you and you alone can release me from this prison tower."

To which Niniane, kissing him tenderly, replied: "My dearest, have no fear. I shall be with you nearly all the time."

Niniane, true to her word, spent the better part of every day and night by the Wizard's side. Though he could not move from the spot, she was able to come and go freely. This arrangement pleased her, the way a new game pleases a child, for a while. But in time she wearied of it and would have released him gladly, for she realized it was cruel to keep him always a prisoner, no matter how often she might share his confinement.

Though with his help she tried to set him free, her efforts were unsuccessful. The spell she had employed so casually turned out to be powerful beyond measure. In the end, it proved unbreakable.

Meanwhile, the King and his subjects were exceedingly distressed by the Wizard's disappearance. Several years passed, yet no one gave up the hope that Merlin would someday return to court, and Arthur's knights rode far and wide, seeking some clue to the mystery of his whereabouts.

Then one day, having searched for many years in vain, Sir Gawain was riding through the forest of Broceliande when he thought he heard a voice addressing him by name. Surveying the area, he could not discover the source of the faint sound, and telling himself it must have been merely the rustling of the wind in the trees, he began to ride away. But the voice came again, louder than before, saying:

"Do not grieve for me, Gawain. What must be, must be."

Whereupon the knight reined in his horse and demanded to know who had spoken to him.

He was answered by a soft, mocking laugh. "Can you have

forgotten me so soon, Gawain?" inquired the voice. "Why then the world must be a truly faithless place. When I served the King, I was given to believe that everyone loved me. I must have been deceived, for it seems I have already become a stranger to Gawain, the most faithful knight in Arthur's kingdom."

At which Gawain, in great excitement, exclaimed, "O Master Merlin, now I recognize your voice! I beg of you, come forth that I may see your face."

"No one may see my face," the Magician told him. "And this is the last time anyone will hear my voice. In fact, no one will ever reach this spot again—not even you, Gawain."

"But surely you shall venture forth someday," declared Gawain.

"Not so," said the Wizard sadly. "The truth is, I am a prisoner—forced to remain where I am for all time. Only she whose power keeps me here may come and go as she pleases; she alone can see me and speak to me."

Gawain expressed great astonishment at these tidings. Then, suddenly overwhelmed with pity for his friend, he said, "It grieves me indeed to think you are not free."

"It is sad," the Magician agreed. "But such is my fate. However much it pains me to think I must stay here forever, it is beyond my power to escape."

Whereupon the knight begged to know how Merlin—the wisest of men—had gotten himself into such a fix as that which he was in.

The Wizard chuckled drily. "The wisest of men is also the greatest of fools, Gawain. I love another better than I love myself. And because of this, I have been enchanted by my own magic. For I taught my beloved the art of sorcery and gave her all the powers I possessed."

Gawain beseeched Merlin to reveal the name of his enchantress, declaring, "Surely I can persuade her to let you go, for pity's sake!"

The Wizard was only too happy to reveal Niniane's name to Gawain. "But," he cautioned, "do not think that by appealing to her, you can in any way alter my fate. Niniane deeply regrets the folly of her deed and would be the first to free me if she could. However, the spell she bound me with was more powerful than anyone can conceive, and her efforts to liberate me from it have all failed miserably."

After a pause, the Wizard continued, "Still, do not grieve for me. Niniane is ever faithful; few days or nights ever pass that she is not by my side. And at these times she always gives me freely of her love and strives, for my sake, to hide the sadness that is forever in her heart."

Though he felt grateful for Niniane's devotion and pleased that Merlin enjoyed her company, Gawain, being only human, could not help weeping inwardly to think that his friend would never be free. Nor could he keep from thinking how wretched his fellow knights would be when they heard of the Magician's fate and realized that they would never lay eyes on him again. Everyone would grieve, but most of all, the King. For Arthur had been raised by Merlin, and until recently, the Wizard had guided his every deed.

Being only human, Gawain was also saddened by the fact that Merlin had chosen to bestow his magical powers upon so questionable a creature as Niniane rather than pass them on to Arthur, his lifelong charge and faithful protégé. Gawain, believing as he did in the King and being so devoted to his sacred cause, could not, for the life of him, see any wisdom in the decision. The more he thought about it, the more it seemed to him that the Wizard had behaved quite foolishly.

Merlin did not try to justify his actions to Gawain, for he was aware that the ways of wizards are beyond the comprehension of human beings. And so he merely charged the knight to convey his blessings to the King and Queen and all the noble knights and ladies and people of the kingdom.

Gawain sadly took his leave of the Magician. He made his way out of the enchanted forest and soon arrived, with a sinking heart, at Camelot. There he described his encounter with the Wizard, faithfully repeating all that had passed between them. Whereupon the King wept openly, and everyone was wretched, just as Gawain had foreseen.

As the Wizard had predicted, no one ever saw or spoke to him again, not even the King. And in the troubled years that followed, Arthur would have done almost anything for an opportunity to consult with Merlin, however briefly.

But that was not to be.

The Wizard had cast away his wand. And though there were many who, like Gawain, perceived only foolishness in the deed, they were all mistaken. Contrary to popular belief, Merlin had not squandered his powers heedlessly nor been foolish in failing to entrust them to the King. For the Wizard's powers were far too dangerous to be entrusted to men, even such men as Arthur and his knights, who were inspired by the loftiest intentions. Had Merlin's powers been bestowed on him, Arthur would have felt compelled to try and rule the world with them, and because this is not the proper task of men, his efforts would not have been successful. In fact, they would have caused more pain and suffering than anyone can conceive.

And so the Magician gave over his powers to Niniane, knowing that she, being a fairy-child, would never dream of interfering with the natural order of things. Indeed, she would not even stop to consider the possible uses of the powers she received. No, being a fairy-child, innocent of ambition and greed, Niniane would take the gift that was powerful beyond all thought and use it—purely for her own amusement—to bewitch the first person she happened to see.

※

Without Merlin's magic to sustain it, the Round Table was beset with problems and finally succumbed to the fate common to all worldly things. And so, although the great achievements of Arthur and his knights are felt even to the present day, the kingdom they established has long since perished and faded into memory.

Yet the spirit of those times lives on, for somewhere, deep in the heart of the forest, beneath an eternally flowering whitethorn bush, the Wizard is still waiting—unheard and unseen.

ACKNOWLEDGEMENTS

To the Medievalist scholar and writer, Heinrich Zimmer, I owe a great debt of gratitude; his work has been an inspiration and guide. Among the other sources I consulted, both ancient and modern, anonymous and signed, I relied particularly on Alfred Lord Tennyson's poetry. I especially wish to thank Frances Foster, my editor, for her wisdom and patience; without her I would have long ago lost faith.

ABOUT THE AUTHOR

Winifred Rosen's interest in the Arthurian tales dates back to a childhood love of myths and legends. She has written many books, among them *Cruisin for a Bruisin* (a highly praised first novel), *Dragons Hate To Be Discreet* (a picture-book illustrated by Edward Koren), and three stories about the exploits of a small girl named Henrietta (illustrated by Kay Chorao). Her stories and articles have appeared in *Harper's Magazine* and *McCalls*. She grew up in New York and now lives on the eastern shore of Long Island.